A LATIN PASSION

BY
KATHRYN ROSS

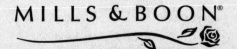

MILLS & BOON®

First published in Great Britain 2004
Harlequin Mills & Boon Limited,
Eton House, 18-24 Paradise Road, Richmond, Surrey TW9 1SR

© Kathryn Ross 2004

ISBN 0 263 83740 8

Set in Times Roman 10½ on 12 pt.
01-0504-49232

Printed and bound in Spain
by Litografía Rosés, S.A., Barcelona

Lucas reached out and caught hold of her arm as she made to turn away. 'Haven't you forgotten something?'

'I don't think so.' Her heart seemed to slam against her chest as she looked back at him, her green eyes wide in her face. Was he going to kiss her? The thought was enough to send her blood pressure soaring.

'Your handbag.' He smiled and picked up her bag from the floor beside her. She couldn't believe that she had nearly forgotten it! It showed the state of her mind.

She took it from him, feeling flustered and wondering if he realised she had thought he meant a kiss. 'Thank you.' She reached again for the door handle.

'Milly?'

She looked round at him, wondering what she had forgotten this time. And that was when he leaned closer and kissed her. It was just a light touch of his lips against hers, but the sensation sent wild forces of desire shooting through her. In that instant she wanted to move closer, give herself up to the sheer pleasure of his caresses.

Kathryn Ross was born in Zambia, where her parents happened to live at that time. Educated in Ireland and England, she now lives in a village near Blackpool, Lancashire. Kathryn is a professional beauty therapist, but writing is her first love. As a child she wrote adventure stories, and at thirteen was editor of her school magazine. Happily, ten writing years later DESIGNED WITH LOVE was accepted by Mills & Boon®. A romantic Sagittarian, she loves travelling to exotic locations.

Recent titles by the same author:

A SPANISH ENGAGEMENT
THE ITALIAN MARRIAGE
BLACKMAILED BY THE BOSS

CHAPTER ONE

WHAT was that old proverb...? Something about keeping your friends close but your enemies even closer...Penny mused as she walked into the head offices of Lucas Shipping. Well, this was her first step into the rival camp and it felt strangely liberating. At least she was doing something constructive, not just sitting waiting for the axe to fall, as her father seemed intent on doing.

A blast of cold air washed over her skin as she went from the tropical Caribbean heat into the air-conditioned foyer, and a shiver ran through her...but whether it was from the cold or the thought of what her father would say if he knew she was here, she didn't know. A few weeks ago, when she had phoned him and voiced the idea of approaching Lucas personally, appealing for more time to pay what was owed, her father had gone almost apoplectic with rage. 'Lucas is the devil incarnate,' he had bellowed.

'But, Dad, you don't really know that,' Penny had insisted softly. 'It was Lucas's father that you had trouble with, and he's dead now. Maybe his son will be better.'

'You can be very naïve sometimes, Penny,' her father had grated angrily. 'Lucas Darien is just like his father, and I'll tell you this: I'd rather go under than ask a member of that family for any favours.'

Penny could just have left things. After all, it was really nothing to do with her; this was her father's business. She had her own career to think about, and as manageress of a beauty spa on board one of the world's biggest lux-

ury cruise liners she was too far away to do anything
anyway. However, a few phone calls later she had heard
her father's anger turn to depression and she had known
that she cared too much about him not to try to step into
the breach. If she'd had enough money she would have
tried to bail him out herself, but the next best thing had
been to ask for leave from work and fly out to Lucas
Darien's head office in Puerto Rico. Maybe her father
was too proud to ask for help, but Penny wasn't.

Okay, maybe the estate had to go…maybe it was time
her father retired. The sugar industry had been going
through a bad patch, and he had been struggling for a
long time to make the estate pay, but surely he didn't
have to lose their family home as well as all their land?
That house had been handed down through three gener-
ations of their family…it was far too precious to let go
without a fight…even if that did mean humbling herself
before the enemy.

'Can I help you?' The receptionist looked up enquir-
ingly as she approached. She was a young woman in her
early twenties, with ash-blonde hair and a slightly ha-
rassed expression in her blue eyes.

'I'm here to see Lucas Darien,' Penny said with brisk
confidence, as if she had every right to see the man
straight away, sidestepping the little fact that she had no
appointment and knew that the man's time was like gold
dust.

'Oh, you must be Mildred Bancroft, Mr Darien's new
PA.' The woman's whole demeanour suddenly seemed
to lighten, and she smiled at Penny warmly. 'Gosh, am
I glad to see you…' Before Penny could say anything
the phone next to them rang and the woman turned away
to pick it up. 'Excuse me a moment…'

Penny was left in a quandary. If she owned up straight

away to the fact that she wasn't Mildred, the new PA, she probably wouldn't get past the reception and wouldn't see Lucas Darien today. She had already phoned twice, trying to make an appointment, and had been told she'd have to wait until the end of the month. Her father didn't have that much time to spare. He had already been warned that an eviction order for the twenty-fifth of this month was likely.

'Oh, hi.' The receptionist giggled at whatever was being said to her at the other end of the line. 'No, things are getting better around here now; the cavalry has finally arrived in the shape of the new PA, so that should take some of the pressure off me...thank God. Yes, I can make dinner tonight—'

'Shauna.' A deep voice boomed from the inner office...a voice that was unquestionably disgruntled. 'Will you please get me the files I asked for half an hour ago?'

'Got to go, Paul.' Shauna hurriedly put the phone down and grimaced at Penny. 'That's the boss,' she hissed. 'But don't worry, his bark is worse than his bite...he's quite nice, really.'

'I'd like them today, Shauna, if that wouldn't be too much trouble,' the voice continued in an even fiercer tone.

'Coming, Mr Darien.' Shauna flushed bright pink. 'He's not in a very good mood recently,' she whispered to Penny as she searched through a pile of papers that were sitting next to her in an untidy heap. 'His girlfriend broke up with him a few weeks ago, then his PA left to get married, and he's been snowed under with work...what with trying to organise things here and sort through his late father's business affairs. I'm having to do more and more...'

'Really?' Penny murmured. It was good to know that

the enemy was having his fair share of problems, and she couldn't help hoping the guy was absolutely miserable. He deserved it after the way he and his family had treated her father. She watched as Shauna started to rummage through the papers with increasingly nervous fingers.

'Where the heck did I put those files?' she wailed under her breath. 'I had them a moment ago. You can't see them, can you? They're in a green folder.'

Penny couldn't help liking this girl, with her dizzy manner and careless chatter. 'Is that them over there?' She pointed to a shelf behind, where two green folders sat next to a cup and saucer on a silver tray.

'Thank heavens for that!' Shauna exclaimed. 'Whoops…I forgot his coffee and it's cold now…another bad mark for me…'

'Well, you can't do everything,' Penny said sympathetically.

'No…' The woman smiled at her gratefully. 'I'm so glad you are here.'

The words were said in such a heartfelt fashion that Penny started to feel a bit guilty that she was not Mildred, the perfect new PA.

'Shauna, what is taking you so long?' Lucas Darien appeared in the doorway, one expensively shod foot tapping impatiently.

Penny's gaze went from that black shiny shoe up over the dark business suit. He was very tall and lean, and yet he had a powerful breadth to his shoulders. Her gaze locked with the dark intensity of his eyes and a frisson of shock surged through her. Lucas Darien was not at all what she had been expecting. The man was absolutely gorgeous. He was probably about thirty-six, he had melting dark eyes and a ruggedly handsome face; his jaw was firm and square, giving the impression of strength and determination, yet his lips had a sensual curve. She wondered what it would be like to be kissed by those lips…

The though sent further shock waves through her and she mentally pulled herself up. Okay, he was attractive…so attractive that he probably wouldn't be out of place playing some macho romantic lead in a movie. But she couldn't let herself forget exactly why she was here. This was Lucas Darien, her father's enemy, not some heart-throb off a movie set.

'This is Mildred Bancroft, Mr Darien,' Shauna said quickly. 'Your new PA.'

'Really?' Surprise registered in his dark eyes. 'You're not what I was expecting.' His gaze swept over her in an almost brutally assessing way that made heat run rampantly through her. How dared he look at her like that? And what did he mean by that statement?

'You are not what I was expecting either,' she murmured, tipping her chin up defiantly.

'What were you expecting?' he asked immediately.

The question took her by surprise, as did the sudden softening of his tone, the smile that played around the dark eyes.

'Well…' She shrugged. In truth she had been expecting him to look more like his father. She had met Lucas's father twice. He had been tall and handsome, but that was where the similarity ended. Lawrence Darien had possessed cool English looks: pale blond hair, pale blue eyes and an aristocratic nose down which he had seemed to peer rather contemptuously. No, Lucas was nothing like his cold, autocratic father…obviously he took after his Spanish mother. Maybe there was some hope that he would be more compassionate than his father…

'Well?' Lucas prompted her, and she realised he was still waiting for an answer.

'You're younger than I expected,' Penny improvised hastily. If she told him who she was before she got into his office, she ran the risk of being shown the door before she could have her say.

'Strange, I was going to say exactly the same thing to you.' Lucas smiled. 'From the CV that the agency sent me, I expected you to be at least fifty.'

Penny felt herself blushing wildly. Obviously he knew she wasn't Mildred Bancroft. 'Eh…well…I can explain…'

'Shauna, bring us through a coffee when you have a minute.' Lucas cut across her to instruct his receptionist, who seemed mesmerised by their exchange.

'Come through into my office.' He stood back and waved Penny through to the inner sanctum.

This was very promising, Penny thought with a smile. He knew she wasn't his PA, but he was still going to give her some of his time.

'Thank you.' She gave him the benefit of her sweetest smile as she passed him in the doorway. He didn't respond, which was somewhat unusual.

Penny was an attractive woman, twenty-eight, with long golden blonde hair, wide green eyes, and a petite figure that curved in all the right places. She was used to men smiling back at her. Persuading this man to treat her father leniently was not going to be easy, she acknowledged grimly.

The office was dark after the brightness of the outer reception. It took a moment for her eyes to adjust to the gloom. The walls were lined with bookshelves. The central desk was awash with files, and behind that were filing cabinets, their drawers wide open as if someone had been searching for something. Another desk in the far corner was covered in boxes that were filled with books and files. It looked as if Lucas Darien had recently disturbed a robbery in progress...either that or he was desperately in need of clerical help.

He motioned her towards the leather chair opposite his and watched as she sat. It wasn't lost on her that there was a brief flicker of interest in his dark eyes as she crossed long shapely legs. At least he wasn't completely immune to her. She had selected her pale green dress very carefully this morning, with the knowledge that it emphasised her curvy figure and had a small split at the front that was teasingly provocative. Penny had figured that if she was going to throw herself on the mercy of her father's enemy she needed all the help she could get.

'Obviously your CV isn't entirely accurate...Ms Bancroft.' He sat down behind the desk and leaned back in his chair to survey her through slightly narrowed eyes.

The statement took Penny by surprise; she had thought he had already figured out that she wasn't Mildred Bancroft. Before she could formulate her reply he was proceeding briskly.

'Let's see...there was ten years at Danovate...five years as PA to Sir Gordon Marsden...then your last job, three years as PA to Lieutenant Colonel Montgomery Cliff in Barbados?' One dark eyebrow rose. 'Unless you started work at the age of ten, I'd say something doesn't add up, Ms Bancroft.'

The sarcasm in his tone grated on her sensitive nerves. 'Or may I call you Mildred?' He leaned forwards suddenly, as if intently interested in hearing her answer.

There was something about his manner, or maybe it was the way his eyes seemed to linger on the softness of her lips, that made her nerves drop into freefall. 'Eh...well, you see, the thing is... You can call me Mildred if you like, but really...my name...' She was starting to sound as if she suffered from a bad speech impediment. Pull yourself together, Pen, she told herself crossly. Tell him who you are and how worried you are about your father. Damn it, cry if you have to…

'Good.' He didn't give her the chance to finish her sentence, just sat back with a satisfied smile. 'Mildred it is, then.' He drummed his fingers on the walnut desk. To Penny's overwrought nerves the noise sounded like a drum roll prior to an execution. She really needed to tell Lucas the truth now. Prolonging this misapprehension was just getting in the way of her reason for being here.

'You see, the thing is, Mildred, as long as you are up to the job here I'm prepared to overlook a slight exaggeration with your qualifications.' The drum roll seemed to be getting louder. 'As you can probably tell, I'm desperately short of staff here. So we'll give it a two-week trial, shall we?'

'Actually, Lucas, we are at cross purposes here,' Penny plunged in. 'I feel I must tell you—'

'Really, Mildred, I don't want or need to know your explanation about the CV. You obviously impressed the agency, because they have said you are worth waiting for, and they have a terrific reputation, so that is good enough for me. If you could just start as soon as possible that would be great.'

Shauna shouldered her way in with a tray of coffee. 'We really need an extra pair of hands around here, don't we, Shauna?' Lucas said jovially.

'Oh, yes.' Shauna nodded and smiled at Penny. 'Helen…that's Mr Darien's last PA…well, she left without giving proper notice. And things have been crazy around here.' She nodded towards the desk behind her. 'All those boxes need sorting out and I can't do everything—'

'Yes, okay, Shauna.' Lucas hastily cleared a space on his desk and then reached to take the tray from her. 'Better get back to your desk now, and hold my calls for a while until I'm finished talking to Mildred.'

As the door closed behind the woman Lucas smiled wryly. 'Poor Shauna has been struggling to cope.'

'Yes, so I noticed.'

'This office is always busy; we deal with major businesses in the West Indies, and ship imports and exports from different islands. On top of that we now have my father's business to sort out, as he died six months ago and his affairs were not quite in order.'

'I'm sorry,' Penny murmured, for some reason feeling obliged to offer her condolences.

'My father was a property developer,' Lucas swept on, as if she hadn't spoken. 'And he had a large portfolio of investment properties which have all been passed down to me.'

'Lucky you.' Penny tried to keep the edge out of her voice. His father had been a charlatan.

'Mmm…but it's not as straightforward as it sounds. I've recently had to dispense with the services of my late father's solicitor—due to the fact that he was acting like a used-car salesman crossed with a Rottweiler. So, the boxes you see on that table, plus the cabinets behind me…along with two other rooms full of documentation at my home…have all been transferred from my father's office, and I'm trying to sort through the chaos myself. Which is where you come in. I'd like you to sort through the debris, filing and organising—'

'Lucas, I feel we have got off on the wrong foot here,' Penny cut across him impatiently. 'You see, Shauna misunderstood the situation when I came into the office. I really came—'

'Do you take milk and sugar?' Lucas asked her smoothly.

'Just milk,' Penny answered distractedly. Why wouldn't he listen to her? she wondered angrily.

'You see, the thing is that a number of my father's documents have gone astray—some very important ones at that. Deeds and other documentation for an old plantation house on Arbuda... You probably haven't heard of the island. It's tiny—just south of the British Virgin Islands.'

'Yes, I've heard of it.' Penny felt a tingle of uneasiness; of course she had heard of Arbuda, it was the island where she had grown up, and it sounded as if he was talking about her father's estate. 'You've lost the deeds to a plantation house?' she ventured cautiously.

'Well, they are not lost, exactly. They are somewhere amidst the chaos.' He waved a hand expansively to indicate the boxes and the cabinets behind him. 'But I need to find them pretty quickly. My father was in the process of repossessing the estate when he died. He had been holding the deeds as collateral because the old guy who lives there, William Kennedy, had owed him money for years. They used to be business partners, but my father had problems with the guy and dissolved the partnership. He told me that out of sentiment he let the debt ride for longer than he should. Kennedy is a bit of a no-hoper, by all accounts. Better that he leaves the place before he gets any further into debt.'

'Really?' Penny could hear her tone hardening. How dared he talk about her father like that? A no-hoper, indeed! Who the hell did Lucas Darien think he was? Her father had worked hard all his life...he was a decent, honest man...unlike his father. Lawrence Darien had been nothing more than a pirate...luring her father onto the rocks of bankruptcy and then trying to steal his land. The worst thing her father had ever done was to go into partnership with that man. It had ruined him financially and spiritually.

'Unfortunately I can't proceed with the repossession order until I find some of the relevant documentation,' Lucas continued, totally oblivious to the fact that Penny was rigid with fury. 'And if I don't find the documentation within the next two or three weeks my father's plans for the place are down the tubes.'

'What were your father's plans for the place?' Penny asked, trying not to sound too interested.

'He owned the neighbouring beachfront property, and there are plans for one hundred houses to go up there. William Kennedy's estate would provide vital access from the main road out to the beachfront development.'

They were going to build one hundred houses along that unspoilt coastline! Penny felt as if her heart had jumped into her mouth. She felt totally sick. All right, she no longer lived in Arbuda. Most of her time was spent at sea. But when she was given leave she always went home…loved her weeks of solitude, just walking and lapping up the scenery. The countryside around her family home was among some of the most unspoilt and beautiful in the Caribbean. It was a natural habitat for rare species of flora and fauna. How the hell had Lawrence Darien managed to get planning permission for one hundred houses?

'Unfortunately the building permission for the land runs out in a month's time, so if we don't make a start before then permission will be revoked due to a change of administration in the planning department in Arbuda.'

'You mean your father greased somebody's palm in

the planning office but that person is no longer there?' Penny murmured in a brittle tone.

'Probably.' Lucas shrugged. 'Anyway, we can't start the building work without the access through Kennedy's land, and if we don't get that within the next few weeks the whole idea is out the window.'

'What a shame.' Penny's tone was dry.

'Yes…isn't it?' Lucas took a sip of his coffee and regarded her steadily over the rim of the cup. 'So, you see, the sooner you can start sifting through the files and boxes the more chance I have of finishing my father's last project.'

Penny didn't say anything to that—her mind was working overtime. If those documents weren't found before the end of the month then the building wouldn't go ahead…plus it would stall her father's eviction from the land.

Could she continue with this pretence of being Mildred Bancroft, find the documents and then misappropriate them? All she would have to do was hide them somewhere, giving her father a few weeks' leeway until the danger had passed. The idea slipped surreptitiously into her mind.

But that would be dishonest, a little voice argued sharply, and she was not a dishonest person. Plus the real Mildred could turn up at any moment, exposing her as a fraud.

Then again, Lucas's father had been dishonest in his dealings with her father—plus he had obtained building permission fraudulently. She would only be helping to put that right.

In fact, if she misappropriated the documents for her father's property she would be helping to conserve an area of outstanding natural beauty, as well as buying time for her father. In a few weeks he would be harvesting the sugar cane and he would have enough money to make an interim payment towards clearing his debt. Okay, it was just prolonging his time on the estate, but it was better than giving up.

'So, when do you think you can start?' Lucas asked her suddenly.

Penny took a deep breath. She could probably manage to fake a few days as a PA. She had secretarial skills, and the management course she had taken before taking over the running of the beauty spa would stand her in good stead. 'How about straight away?' she answered quickly, before she could change her mind.

CHAPTER TWO

THEY said that night was the mother of council, and it was probably true—because all that night Penny tossed and turned and regretted the wild impulse that had made her pretend to be Lucas Darien's PA.

It had been a crazy thing to do. Mildred Bancroft could turn up tomorrow, and then she would be in deep trouble. Lucas could call the police; she could be prosecuted for fraud. Penny stared up at the fan that whirled around on the ceiling of her hotel bedroom and felt sick with apprehension.

All her life she had played by the rules... And now, due to one moment of insanity, she could be in deep trouble. But she had just been so incensed by Lucas's cavalier remarks about her father...a no-hoper, indeed! Her father had been a successful businessman before getting involved with Lawrence Darien. And as for Lawrence going easy on her father out of sentiment because they had once been partners...well, frankly there was more truth in one of the brothers Grimm fairytales than there was in that!

Lawrence had been out to ruin her father. The feud between the men went back years, to a time when they had been successful business partners. And the reason they had first fallen out was not over money, but over the love of a woman...and the woman had been Penny's mother.

Before she had married Penny's father, Clara had dated Lawrence Darien—had been head over heels in love with him, by all accounts. Then she had discovered he already had a wife in Puerto Rico, and a son! Clara had been devastated and had sought solace in the arms of William Kennedy. Two months later they had married.

Lawrence had been furious and had disappeared back to Puerto Rico, vowing revenge and leaving their business dealings unfinished.

Her father had gone back to running his estate and had tried to put Lawrence Darien out of his mind. Penny had been born twelve months later and the couple had seemed very happy. Penny had enjoyed an idyllic childhood, and if Lawrence Darien was mentioned it had only been briefly in passing. Yet Penny suspected that her father had never been completely sure of his wife's love for him, that there had always been that knowledge that he had captured the beautiful Clara by default, that she had really only married him on the rebound.

Then, when she was sixteen, Penny's mother had died and everything had changed.

Lawrence Darien had turned up at the funeral. He had offered his profuse condolences to her father and the two men had seemed to rekindle their friendship...and later their old business ties. Their partnership had never been legally terminated, so it had been easy to pick up where they had left off. And her father had found himself investing in land and dealing in property that sometimes he hadn't even seen.

Penny had been uneasy about the reunion. She remembered the two men sitting out on the porch until late at night drinking... She remembered the hard glint in Lawrence's eyes whenever her mother's name was mentioned. When she had pointed this out to her father he had waved it away as her imagination. But it hadn't been her imagination. Lawrence had systematically and ruthlessly set out to ruin her father. And by the time William had realised the fact it was too late.

Her father's judgement had been flawed not because he was a no-hoper or stupid, but because he had been in a state of grief. And Lawrence had taken advantage of that. Had even managed to get hold of the deeds of their estate. Now, almost thirteen years down the line, even after death he was about to exact his last and terrible revenge. The loss of the estate would kill her father; she felt sure of that.

Penny tossed and turned in her bed. If there was an opportunity to even the score wasn't she right to take it?

She stared up at the fan on the ceiling. She remembered the last time she had seen Lawrence Darien. She remembered asking him why he had treated her father so ruthlessly. He had smiled at her with cold contempt. 'I always settle old scores,' he had murmured, before turning his back on her.

Well, wasn't it her turn to settle the score once and for all? she asked herself angrily. For her mother, who had been badly hurt at that man's hands, as well as her father...

Finally, as dawn broke outside, Penny drifted into sleep. But her slumber was beleaguered by wild, terrifying dreams. Lawrence Darien was pursuing her through dark corridors. 'If you think you can fool a member of my family then you are wrong,' he told her when finally he caught up with her.

The touch of his hand on her shoulder made her blood curdle, but as he swung her around to face him something happened. The cold, angry face didn't belong to Lawrence—it was Lucas who was holding her.

'There is a price to pay for deception,' he murmured, his eyes on her lips. And suddenly the feeling of the dream changed from deeply troubled to intensely sensual. 'I hope you can afford to pay...'

'What is your price?' she asked huskily.

Then he leaned towards her and his lips crushed against hers in a kiss that was so incredibly passionate it was mind-blowing. Her senses reeled, as if she had just been pushed out of a plane at thirty thousand feet. She kissed him back, wanting so much more, wanting his hands on her body...

The shrill ring of the alarm made her sit upright. Her heart was thundering...and she felt incredibly turned on. That was the weirdest dream she had ever had. Even now the erotic intensity of it was deeply disturbing...so real it seemed to mock her somehow.

She pushed the covers of the bed back and went through to the bathroom to run a shower. Obviously she had eaten too late last night...or maybe it was the heat of this room. The air-conditioning didn't seem to be working properly and the fan was ineffectual.

If she was going to stay here for another night she should report it at the reception desk. Should she stay another night? Should she go through with this deception? Or should she fly home and comfort her father...help him pack up a lifetime of belongings, ready to move. Her company had told her she could take up to five weeks' leave, so she had time to organise the move.

The thought made a shiver of anger run through her. Why should her father move from his home? It was outrageous. Why should Lawrence Darien get away with what he had done? No, she would stay here and risk playing the part of Mildred Bancroft for today at least...

Maybe she would be lucky and find the papers straight away...put them somewhere Lucas would never think of looking and then fly back to Miami to join her ship.

Lucas Darien might never connect her with the missing papers…might never find out who she really was. And, even if he did, mislaying papers was hardly major fraud.

'Mildred…? Mildred…? Mildred, are you deaf?'

Penny looked up as she suddenly realised that Lucas was talking to her. 'Oh, sorry! I was miles away.'

'What on earth were you thinking about?' Lucas perched on the edge of her desk and grinned at her.

His closeness was deeply unsettling, as was the way his eyes crinkled at the edges when he smiled at her. 'I was thinking…'

Her mind groped for an excuse. She could hardly tell him that she hadn't recognised her own name! Or that she had been thinking that expecting to find the missing papers in one working day had been wildly optimistic. She had been in this office since nine, hadn't even bothered taking a lunch break and it was now time to go home…and there was no sign of the missing papers and depressingly she had only cleared two filing cabinets.

'I was just thinking that it must be nearly dinner time…my stomach is starting to feel like my throat's been cut,' she improvised.

'I'm not surprised. You've had no lunch and you've been working very hard.' Lucas looked with approval at the way she had neatly and methodically catalogued everything she had taken from the cabinets. 'You are very thorough.'

Penny shrugged. She was meticulous and organised in her running of the spa; she did accounts, kept track of stock, dealt with clients and staff. Putting Lucas's office in order was relatively simple, if somewhat time-consuming.

'You better call it a day now, though,' Lucas said as he glanced at his watch. 'Shauna left half an hour ago.'

'Did she?' Penny was surprised she hadn't heard the other woman leave. 'I didn't realise it was that late.'

Lucas grinned. 'She had a hot date, and I didn't have the heart to tell her she was actually leaving early...she has put in a lot of overtime these last few days.'

Lucas could be very nice, Penny thought hazily as her eyes drifted over him, and he looked extremely handsome in that dark suit. She wondered if he worked out to get that superbly fit physique, or if it just came naturally to him. Her gaze moved towards the penetrating intensity of his dark eyes, to the soft curve of his lips, and suddenly she found herself remembering her dream this morning...the sensual way he had kissed her. Heat licked its way through her entire body at the memory.

Hastily she pulled her gaze away from his face. That dream had been absurd, she told herself as she transferred her attention to the last pile of papers on her desk. Being attracted to Lucas Darien would be asking for trouble. Behind all that charm he was probably just like his father...he was probably married as well... Although hadn't Shauna said something about him not being in a good mood due to his relationship with his girlfriend ending? So maybe he wasn't married? Not that she cared.

'By the way, Mildred, I need some details from you so I can put you in the system—you know, the usual kind of thing...your bank account number so I can organise your salary payments direct to your bank account, and—'

'If you don't mind I'd like to wait until my two-week trial period is over before you put me into the system,' Penny cut across him swiftly. She was amazed at how coolly self-assured she sounded, when in reality her heart was starting to beat with fear and dread.

Lucas regarded her steadily, his dark eyes never wavering from her face. 'Why is that, then? Are you thinking you might not want to stay?'

'No...' Penny tried to smile. She had to play this very carefully, because if Lucas found out she was an impostor things could turn very nasty, very quickly. 'I'd just like to keep things on a casual footing until we decide to make my job permanent.'

'You mean our trial period is a two-way street?' Lucas shrugged. 'That's fair enough...' He grinned. 'I'd better be on my best behaviour, then, if I want to keep you.'

Penny was intensely tempted to relax and grin back at him, make an equally jesting remark. It would be all too easy to be taken in by his amiable manner, she thought hazily as she looked into the warmth of his eyes...all too easy to respond to him and relax her guard, and then...then he'd discover she wasn't really Mildred Bancroft and all hell would break loose. So instead she just nodded her head. 'Yes, good idea,' she remarked, and smiled lightly before turning away from him to continue going through the remainder of the papers in front of her.

'So how about if I start by offering you a lift home?' Lucas continued.

'That really isn't necessary...but thank you anyway.' Once again she gave him a very brief, cool smile before continuing on with her work.

But she was only pretending to be deeply engrossed in what she was doing; in reality she was intensely aware of his close proximity and she wished he would move away.

'I know it's not necessary, but I'm offering anyway.' Lucas seemed completely undeterred by her frosty responses. 'Whereabouts are you living, Mildred?'

The casual question caused a deep ripple of anxiety inside Penny. She wished she knew something about her namesake. Where was Mildred from? What information did Lucas already possess? She looked up at him, consternation clear in her green eyes. She hated this…she was no good at lying…she was going to be found out. Panic clouded her mind.

Then suddenly the fog lifted and she remembered something Lucas had said when he was interviewing her. Mildred's last job had been three years as PA to Lieutenant Colonel Montgomery Cliff in Barbados. She latched on to the memory in grateful desperation.

'Since leaving Barbados I've been in a state of flux, really. A lot of my possessions are still in storage, so at the moment I'm staying in a hotel here in San Juan.' Considering the only part of the statement that was true was the end bit, it sounded remarkably convincing. Penny found herself marvelling at her own ingenuity.

'So I take it it's not just Lucas Shipping that's on trial? It's Puerto Rico as well?' Lucas hazarded a guess. 'You're not sure you want to stay here?'

Penny nodded, willing to go with that theory and praying he would call a halt to the questions now.

'Well, I don't think you will regret coming to Puerto Rico. It's a truly beautiful island—very exotic, mile after mile of stunning beaches, a rainforest and mountain scenery that is quite breathtaking…plus its people are amongst some of the warmest and most hospitable of the Caribbean.' He grinned, a boyishly teasing grin. 'However, speaking as someone who has lived here most of his life, I'm obviously biased…'

She smiled back at him. 'Obviously.'

'So where are you from originally?'

The follow-up question was unexpected. 'Well, I...' Penny coughed to clear her throat. If she told him she was from Arbuda he was going to put two and two together before very long. 'I'm originally from Barbados.' She stuck to the same island that she was supposed to have worked on...in the hope that it might simplify things and she might remember what she had told him.

'Nice island. It must have been a wonderful place to grow up.'

'Yes...wonderful...' Penny could feel herself growing very hot and uncomfortable.

'Do you still have family in Barbados?'

'Eh...' She coughed again, and caught her breath.

'You okay?' He reached and slapped her on the back as she struggled to regain a lungful of air.

'Fine...thank you...' she wheezed.

He stood up and went to get her a glass of water from the drinking tap just outside the office door. Penny watched him surreptitiously from beneath her eyelashes. Did he have suspicions about her? she wondered. He seemed to be asking a lot of questions.

She had managed to compose herself by the time he returned, but she pretended that she was still short of breath just in case he started to resume his questions. But Lucas didn't pick up where he had left off; he just watched as she sipped the ice-cool water.

'Thank you,' she whispered hoarsely as she put the cup down.

'You're welcome.' He smiled, and then stretched over to switch off the desk lamp beside her. 'Come on, let's get out of here. I think we've both worked hard enough for one day.'

Penny reached for her bag, glad to push her chair back

and stand up. She desperately wanted to get away from him in case more questions were suddenly fired at her.

'Right, well, I'll see you tomorrow morning,' she said briskly.

He glanced over at her with a raised eyebrow. 'It's Saturday tomorrow, Mildred.'

'Is it?' Penny's heart sank. The weekend was the last thing she needed right now. It was vital she found those files before Mildred turned up and blew her cover...a two-day break could be disastrous. 'I'd lost track of time,' she murmured.

'Actually, I was going to ask you if you wouldn't mind doing some overtime this weekend?' Lucas asked as he switched off the overhead light and then held the door for her to precede him out of the office. 'The thing is that I really need to find those missing documents, and time is not on my side.'

'Yes, I quite understand.' Penny grabbed the straw gratefully. 'I don't mind doing a bit of overtime at all, Lucas. I've got nothing planned this weekend anyway.'

'Great.' Lucas smiled across at her. 'I'll make it worth your while financially, of course.'

Penny found herself waving a hand in airy dismissal. She couldn't have cared less what Lucas was planning to pay her because she didn't plan on sticking around to take any of his money. 'We'll sort that out at a later date, once I've decided to stay. Or you've decided you *want* me to stay...' she added hastily, not wishing to sound too sure of herself.

'I get the feeling that it's a rare occurrence for employers not to want you to stick around,' Lucas said with a grin as he opened the outer door for her.

'Modesty prevents me from answering that question.' Penny couldn't resist smiling back at him. It sounded as

if he didn't have any suspicions about her at all…that
had just been her guilty conscience. He'd probably just
been making polite conversation when he'd asked her a
few questions about herself. She was going to have to
stop being so edgy around him otherwise he was bound
to suss her out.

'So, where can I drop you?' Lucas asked as he locked
the office door. 'My car is just down the road.'

'I'm going to get the bus, Lucas—'

'Don't be silly.' He strode away from her towards the
entrance to a car park, leaving Penny little option but to
follow.

In one way she was glad to get a lift back; she was
tired and hot… On the other hand Lucas would know
where she was now…would be able to go into the hotel
and enquire about her.

Lucas unlocked a silver-grey Mercedes and she slipped
into the passenger seat. Although it was nearly six, and
the sun was starting to set in a blaze of orange and pink
light, the heat of the day was still intense. The cool air
from the conditioning unit in the car was blissful.

'So, where to?' Lucas asked as he pulled the car out
of the side street and into the busy flow of traffic on a
one-way street.

'I'm staying in the old quarter of San Juan.'

'Picturesque down there, isn't it?' Lucas remarked as
he waited for the traffic to move.

'Yes, it's lovely.'

'Which hotel?'

'Casa del Clarinda. It's only a small hotel. It's on—'

'Yes, I know exactly where it is.'

'Oh…' Penny fell silent. She wished he hadn't said
that, because for some reason it made her feel even more
vulnerable. Now she was wondering if he knew the own-

ers... After all it *was* a small hotel, and it was strange
he knew 'exactly' where it was. She imagined him bumping into them in some bar somewhere and saying, *You
have my PA Mildred Bancroft staying with you.* And the
puzzled looks on their faces.

Then he'd start to describe her. *Long blonde hair,
about twenty-eight, green eyes, five foot six....*

Oh, that sounds like Penny Kennedy.

A cold shiver ran through her.

'Is the air-conditioning a bit fierce?' Lucas glanced
across at her.

'No, I'm fine.'

'You're shivering. Wind down the window and let
some warm air in if you want.'

'Thanks.' Lucas Darien didn't miss much, she thought
warily.

The car picked up a bit of speed as the traffic thinned
out, and warm air flowed in, brushing the heavy weight
of her hair back from her face. 'How come you know
where my hotel is?' she asked, trying to sound nonchalant.

'It's got a very good reputation. Everyone knows it.'

It didn't sound as if he knew the owners...relief was
immense.

'I was thinking that tomorrow you should work up at
my house,' Lucas continued casually. 'I have two whole
rooms full of my father's files up there, so the sooner
you can make a start the better.'

Two rooms! It had taken her a whole day to get
through two filing cabinets, so how long would it take
her to get through that lot? she wondered distractedly. By
the sounds of things she would be extremely lucky if she
found those missing files before Mildred Bancroft arrived.

'But don't worry—I'll give you a hand to sort through them,' Lucas continued when she didn't say anything. 'I've got time tomorrow.'

'Oh, really, there is no need,' Penny assured him hastily. The last thing she needed was Lucas watching her every move; it had been bad enough having to share an office with him today.

'We'll get through them quicker with two of us working.'

'I suppose you're right.' There was little else she could say. Penny's heart sank. If he found the documents all this could be for nothing.

Lucas turned left, and the car bumped over the cobbled road as they entered the old quarter of San Juan. Penny knew this area quite well as her ship often pulled into port here. It was an area that was over five hundred years old and had been designated as a world heritage site. Buildings that were Spanish in character flanked the quaint narrow streets; they were painted cool pastel shades and had wrought-iron balustrades, some filled with a profusion of flowers.

'You can drop me here, if you like,' she said as they approached the crossroads that led down to her hotel.

'I'll drop you at the door; it's no problem,' Lucas answered in a tone that brooked no argument. 'What made you decide to come to Puerto Rico, Mildred?' he asked idly as he turned slowly down her road.

'Well…the agency offered me this job and I thought it sounded interesting…' She felt slightly breathless. 'I like to move around…see different places…'

'You're a bit of a free spirit, I take it?' He glanced over at her speculatively.

'Yes, I suppose I am.' At least that was the truth. She

did like travelling—it had been one of the reasons she had applied for a job on a cruise liner.

'That's something we have in common, then.' He pulled up outside her hotel. 'One of the reasons I started a shipping company was my fascination with faraway shores.'

'Did your father help you build up your business?' she asked curiously.

'No, he was never interested in trade on the high seas...just on dry land.'

'And were you involved in his property deals?' She didn't know why she asked him that; curiosity, she supposed. There was a part of her that couldn't help wondering how close he had been to his father and if he knew just how shady the man had been.

'No, I was always too busy with my own business. Why do you ask?'

'I just wondered if you had any idea where we should start looking in those files tomorrow,' she improvised wildly, and was suddenly glad that it was dark and he couldn't see how red her skin had become. She shouldn't have asked that question; it wasn't a good idea to sound too interested in his affairs.

'No...unfortunately I don't.'

'Never mind. I'm sure between us we'll find them tomorrow.' She spoke positively.

'Let's hope so.'

And let's hope I find them first, she added silently as she reached to open the car door. To her surprise Lucas got out and came around to open the door for her. Such old-fashioned courtesy took her aback.

She accepted the hand he offered and stepped out onto the pavement. The touch of his skin against hers sent a strange sensation of intense awareness shooting through her. Abruptly she let go of him.

'Thank you for the lift.' Her voice was primly polite.

'You're welcome.' He grinned. 'It's the least I could do after you've worked so hard, and through your lunch hour.'

The evening air was warm, perfumed by the bougain-villaea and jasmine that cascaded from the balcony of the hotel.

For a moment she stood staring up at him. Lucas Darien was incredibly handsome, she thought hazily. Tall and lean, yet there was that air of latent power about him. Maybe it was the breadth of his shoulders that gave him such a commanding presence, or maybe it was the way he met her eyes with such calm self-assurance. Whatever it was, he seemed to just exude sex appeal.

'I'll pick you up tomorrow morning, about eight-forty-five,' he said quietly.

She was so mesmerised, looking up into the darkness of his eyes, that it took a moment for her to register that him picking her up might not be a good idea. If he was to walk into the hotel and ask for Ms Mildred Bancroft she'd be in deep water.

'It's okay,' she said hastily. 'If you give me your address I'll take a taxi.'

'You like to be independent, don't you?' He smiled. 'But it's no problem. I have to come down to the dock-side in the morning anyway. I have some business to take care of.'

'Oh…but—'

'If I'm running late I'll phone you. What's your room number?'

'Em…I…I can't remember. But, listen, it's just as easy for me to catch a cab and—'

Lucas reached out and tipped her chin upward, so that she was forced to look directly into his eyes again. The contact was brief and light, yet the sensation sent shivers of pandemonium racing through her from nowhere.

'I'll pick you up,' he said firmly. 'Don't worry about your room number—I'm sure the Casa del Clarinda has only one Mildred Bancroft in residence.'

That's what he thinks, Penny reflected in alarm as she watched him walk away from her.

'See you tomorrow, Mildred.'

'Yes…tomorrow…'

Lucas got back into his car, but he didn't drive away immediately. Instead he waited and watched as she turned to walk into the hotel. For a moment she was silhouetted against the light from the foyer. He noticed the shapely curve of her figure in the pale blue dress, the way her hair shone like spun gold. He remembered the way she had looked up at him a moment ago, the way her eyes had been flecked with some deep emotion… She had looked at him like that several times today. It was as if one moment she was deeply distrustful of him…ready to do battle with him…and the next she relaxed and gave him a most breathtakingly beautiful smile.

He would give anything to know exactly what was going on in her mind…

Lucas put the car into gear and pulled away from the sidewalk. The delicate scent of her perfume still lingered in the car, just as the memory of her wide clear green eyes lingered in his mind. There was something about the delectable Ms Bancroft that intrigued him, an air of mystery that needed further investigation…

CHAPTER THREE

PENNY woke at first light and quickly showered and dressed in a lightweight trouser suit that was a pale shade of oyster-pink. She applied a little make-up, to disguise the fact that she hadn't slept very well again, swept her hair back from her face with a clip and then went downstairs to the reception, to see if she could solve the little problem of what would happen when Lucas asked for Ms Bancroft.

Penny's heart sank as she noticed that the woman receptionist who was normally on duty wasn't there. Instead it was the man who had checked her in on her arrival. He was in his early thirties, and had a swarthy complexion and eyes that were boldly assessing. Penny hadn't particularly liked him—had thought he was just a little too interested in her.

'Morning, Ms Kennedy,' he greeted her with a smile as she approached the counter. 'You're up bright and early.'

Penny tried not to notice the male interest in his eyes as they swept over her figure in a rather blatant way, and instead smiled back at him. 'Thought I'd take a stroll before the heat of the day got too intense.'

'Good idea. Have you any special plans for the rest of the day?'

'Actually, I'm going out for the day...with a friend.' She kept her smile in place with great difficulty. Why couldn't the nice woman from last night have been on duty? she wondered with an inner sigh. She wouldn't

34

have asked anything. 'In fact, he should be picking me up in a couple of hours.' She kept her voice light. 'Will you still be on duty?'

'Yes, I'm here until ten.'

'If you'd ring me when he arrives that would be great.' She fixed him with her most winning smile. 'Oh…and I almost forgot,' she said as she made to turn away. 'He'll probably ask for me by the name of Mildred Bancroft. That's my professional name.'

'What profession is that, then?' the man asked immediately, the light of interest rekindled.

'Oh, I do a bit of writing in my spare time, under the name of Mildred Bancroft. That's why I'm in Puerto Rico, actually, to do a spot of research for a book. Perhaps you'd be kind enough to tell the other receptionists, so that if a call comes for Mildred Bancroft they will put it through to my room, or take a message for me? I don't want to miss any important calls from my publisher.'

The receptionist opened his mouth, probably to ask her what she wrote, but Penny wasn't about to start embroidering her tale any further. She'd had enough lies for one day. 'Anyway, I'd better dash,' she said quickly, and pretended to look at her watch. 'The day is flying by, and I won't get my walk if I don't hurry.'

Her heart was thudding unevenly as she stepped outside into the bright sunlight. She hated all these lies. Had the man been convinced? she wondered. In case he hadn't she intended to find a shady spot to wait for Lucas's arrival, waylay him before he had a chance to go into the hotel.

Finding a shady place to sit and wait turned out to be easier than expected. There was a square directly opposite the hotel, and as luck would have it a tiny coffee bar was open. She took a seat in the window, so she could watch for Lucas's car in case he arrived early, and then ordered a cappuccino.

Hopefully she would find the missing files today. Then she would get a flight out of here and put this unpleasant business behind her. Her father need never know that she had meddled in his affairs…it would just be a pleasant surprise for him when the eviction order didn't come through on the twenty-fifth. That was presuming she was successful in finding the documents, and that Mildred Bancroft didn't turn up and ruin everything.

She was on her second cup of coffee when she saw Lucas's car pull up outside the hotel. Hurriedly she put some dollar bills on the table and rushed out without waiting for her change.

'Good morning, Lucas.' She called to him from across the road as he locked his car door. For a moment she thought he hadn't heard her. Then he turned around.

'Morning.' He leaned back against the bonnet of the car and watched as she made her way across towards him.

A warm breeze blew her jacket back, giving a glimpse of a black lacy top that fitted her svelte figure like a second skin. His eyes swept over her, noticing the long length of her legs in the elegant trouser suit and the fact that she was wearing very high heels that were impeding her progress across the cobbled street.

'You're out and about very early this morning.' He grinned at her as she reached his side.

'Thought I'd get a bit of fresh air before the heat of the day closes in.'

'Good idea.' He smiled at her; it was a warm, inviting smile and it made her feel a bit breathless. There was something about Lucas Darien that seemed to set her pulses racing. She tried to tell herself it was just nervous tension, because of all these lies that she was telling, but deep down she knew there was more to it than that. The thing was that she found him dangerously attractive. She knew she shouldn't be drawn to him, that it was a bit like the fascination that a moth felt towards a flame, but she couldn't seem to help herself.

'I always think that the morning is the best part of the day,' Lucas said as he went around to open the passenger door for her.

'Especially when the rest of the time is going to be spent in an office,' she agreed, trying to concentrate on the conversation and not on him.

'Are you wishing you hadn't agreed to overtime this weekend, by any chance?' He grinned.

'No, I don't mind.'

'Well, I promise not to work you too hard today. We'll stop about midday and have a leisurely lunch—how's that?'

'Let's see how far we get through those files before we decide how much time off we can have,' Penny said non-committally.

'If you are trying to impress me with your commitment to work then you are succeeding, Mildred Bancroft,' he said, a glint of humour in his dark eyes. 'Are you always so focused?'

'I try to be.' She got into the car and watched as he walked around to join her. It was true she usually had no problem concentrating on what was important. Trouble was, she seemed to be focusing on the wrong things when she was around him. He was very distracting. And the way he was dressed this morning was even more of a distraction. He was wearing casual clothes today, faded blue jeans and a pale blue T-shirt that seemed to emphasise the wide expanse of his chest and the taut flatness of his stomach. She was willing to bet that beneath that T-shirt there was a toned six-pack.

Swiftly she averted her eyes from him. Don't think about things like that, Penny, she told herself crossly. Keep focused on the reason you're here. Lucas Darien is the enemy.

He got into the car and smiled across at her. She smiled back at him. He had the sexiest eyes, she thought hazily.

'Don't forget your seatbelt,' he said.

'No, of course not.' Hastily she snapped out of her reverie and reached to put it on. Strange thing was, she hadn't felt this strongly attracted to a man in years... The last person who had interested her like this was Nick, and that had ended in total disaster. He had been the reason she had left Arbuda and gone to work at sea.

She had been deeply in love with Nick. They had lived together for over a year and she had been committed to the relationship, had thought he was too. It had come as a hell of a shock to discover he had been seeing someone else behind her back. That all the nights he had said he was working overtime because they were saving up to get married he had in fact been wining and dining another woman. The betrayal had hurt; Penny had sworn nobody would ever get under her skin like that again...ever.

Even though her break-up with Nick had been two years ago it still pained her to think about it. Firmly she switched her attention to the scenery outside. They had left the town behind now, and the powerful car was climbing easily up narrow mountain roads. The countryside was green and tropical—they passed plantations of banana and grapefruit—and the view down over the tumbling greenery towards the turquoise of the sea was spectacular.

Lucas turned the car through a narrow driveway that twisted up through manicured gardens lined with palm trees, before coming to a standstill outside a large colonial-style house. Steps led up to a wide porch, which wrapped around the building and was furnished with wicker furniture and a swing chair that was positioned to give the best view through the trees towards the sea.

The first thing that struck Penny as she climbed out of the car was the silence of the surroundings. All she could hear was the rustle of the warm breeze in the palm trees and the sound of the birds. It reminded her of her father's house in Arbuda.

'You've got a lovely place here,' Penny said as she walked up the steps with him to the veranda.

'It used to be an old coffee plantation house, but previous owners sold it separately from the land many years ago. It had fallen into a bad state of disrepair when I bought it, and needed a lot of work to restore it back to its former beauty, but I think we got there in the end.' He held open the screened door for her and allowed her to precede him into a large hallway.

Penny could see at once that no expense had been spared in restoring the beauty of the place. It had solid wooden floors covered by a Persian rug, and a wide sweeping staircase where a magnificent grandfather clock stood on the turn of the landing. She had a glimpse of a drawing room to the right, with gold and blue furnishings, and to the left a formal dining room with a long polished mahogany table. The house had a comfortable elegance that spoke of bygone days.

'My study is at the back of the house—' Lucas broke off as a door was flung open and a little girl raced down the corridor, closely followed by a black Labrador who barked excitedly.

'Guess what's happened this morning,' the child said eagerly, reaching up so that Lucas would pick her up.

'What's happened?' He obligingly scooped her up into his arms and then glanced over at the dog. 'Be quiet, Flint,' he said sternly, and the animal immediately fell silent, but stood wagging his tail and looking up at his master expectantly. 'So what's all the excitement about?' Lucas asked the child.

'Mrs Gordon was baking a cake and it burnt and black smoke came out of the oven and the smoke alarm rang and she shouted a lot.'

'Sounds like a morning of high excitement.' Lucas grinned over at Penny. 'We never have a dull moment here. Mildred, this is my daughter, Isobel.'

Lucas had a child… Penny was completely taken aback by the discovery. Did that mean he also had a wife? Since Shauna had mentioned his break-up with his girlfriend she had more or less decided he must be single. But she should have known better. He was probably a womaniser, just like his father.

She was aware that the knowledge sent a curious pang of disappointment flooding through her.

The little girl looked over at her with wide, serious eyes. She only looked about six years of age, and she was adorable, with a cute heart-shaped face, straight shiny black hair and eyes that were so dark they looked almost jet-black.

'Hello, Isobel.' Penny smiled at her.

'Hello.' She smiled back.

A woman appeared in the corridor behind them, one hand on her ample hips and a frown marring her rounded face. 'Isobel, come and clear up this mess you've made in the pantry, please.'

'Yes, Mrs Gordon.' Isobel didn't look in the slightest

bit chastened. In fact her eyes danced with mischief and merriment as she slipped down from her father's arms and dutifully headed back towards the other woman.

'I believe you've had a bit of an exciting morning in the kitchen, Mrs Gordon,' Lucas said jovially.

'The thermostat on the oven must be faulty,' the woman said with a shake of her head. 'I've never had such a disaster.' She glared at the black Labrador as he tried to sneak past her to follow Isobel through the door. 'And I've told you that the kitchen is no place for a dog,' she said sternly, pointing a finger at him. 'Out with you.'

Flint backed away and then stood staring at the door dejectedly as it banged closed behind the woman and child.

'And that was Mrs Gordon, my housekeeper...cum nanny,' Lucas said with a smile as he turned to lead the way down a side corridor. 'Don't be misled by her grumpy exterior; the woman is a treasure. Runs the house with smooth efficiency... Well, she usually does.' Lucas grinned. 'I've never known her burn anything before.'

'We all have our off days,' Penny murmured. 'Your wife must be grateful for her help. This is a big house to keep in order.'

'Unfortunately my wife died four years ago.'

'I'm so sorry.' Penny looked over at him in consternation. She felt guilty now, for thinking he was a womaniser like his father.

Lucas opened a door into what would have been a large airy study, but filing cabinets and boxes took up all the available space and practically obscured the French windows that lined one side of the room.

'Told you there was a lot of sorting out to do,' Lucas said as he glanced over and saw the expression on her face.

But Penny wasn't thinking about the files and the amount of work; she was thinking how wrong it felt to be deceiving this man. Guilt was eating through her in waves. Maybe Lucas was nothing like his father…maybe she should come clean and admit exactly who she was?

Before she could say anything the phone on the desk rang and Lucas strode across to pick it up. 'Hi… No, I haven't found them yet. Hopefully they'll turn up today, and we can have William Kennedy out promptly at the end of the month. Then the bulldozers can move in.'

Penny felt herself stiffen as she heard her father's name mentioned in such a cold way.

'I'll ring you and keep you up to date, Salvador. Yes…no problem. How's Maria? Well, give her my love.' Lucas put the phone down and glanced over at her. 'Are you okay?' he asked, and she realised she was standing inside the open door just staring at him.

'Yes…fine.' Hastily she moved away from the door and closed it behind her.

'That was Salvador. He's a family friend as well as my solicitor. His wife is expecting their first child any day now, so it's all excitement over there.'

'I'm surprised he has the time to think about work on a Saturday,' Penny said as she crossed towards the desk.

'Yes, he's a good man. I'm grateful to him for agreeing to take over from my late father's solicitor. That guy was very shifty indeed. I didn't trust him at all.'

Which was probably why his father had employed him, Penny thought wryly. He'd probably deliberately sought the services of a less than scrupulous solicitor.

'So your friend is going to oversee the eviction order on Mr Kennedy?'

'If I can find the relevant documents.'

Penny pretended to be engrossed in clearing a space

on the office desk so that she could begin work. 'Do you have any misgivings about this?' she asked lightly.

'About what?'

'Evicting an old man from his property?' She tried to keep her tone as casual as possible.

Lucas didn't reply immediately, and she glanced over at him, suddenly realising how much she wanted him to say yes. Maybe he didn't know how corrupt his father had been…maybe there were other things besides the dodgy solicitor that were concerning him. And if he admitted that to her she could tell him the truth. They could sit down and talk about this situation in a civilised manner and come to some arrangement that would save her father's house.

He gave a wry smile. 'That's a strange question.'

'Is it?' Panic raced through her as she wondered if she had overstepped the line.

'Yes.' Lucas leaned back against the filing cabinet behind him and fixed her with a look that was deeply probing. 'Why are asking that?'

'I…I just remembered you saying that the man used to be your father's business partner, and I wondered if there was a part of you that regretted having to take such a drastic course of action, that's all.'

'Well, you know what they say, Mildred…there can be no sentiment in business.'

It was the kind of cold, hard answer his father would have given, and Penny felt a wave of disappointment. She wanted to tell him that this wasn't business, that this was a vendetta against an elderly, frail man—a vendetta that his cold-hearted father seemed determined to pursue even after death. But to say as much would be to reveal her hand, and she wasn't sure that was the right thing to do…not after hearing him in action, speaking to his solicitor.

Lucas seemed keen to evict her father, probably because there was a hell of a lot of money riding on this property development. And, as he had just said, there was no sentiment when it came to business. There also seemed very little in the way of ethics or morality either, when it came to the Darien way of doing things.

'Well, I suppose we ought to get started,' she said instead as she took off her jacket and reached for one of the files. To hell with it anyway, she thought as she emptied it out onto her desk and ruthlessly started to rake through the contents, searching for her father's deeds. Modern-day life seemed to be dog eat dog…she might as well just get in amongst the pack and make the most of this opportunity. It might be the only chance her father had of surviving.

The hours seemed to fly by after that. File followed file, and still there was no sign of the missing papers. When Lucas suggested breaking for lunch Penny shook her head. 'We need to get on. Time is against us as it is,' she murmured.

'Well, I'll tell you what—we'll have a working lunch, but on one condition only.'

'What's that?' She glanced across at him.

He smiled. 'That you stay and have dinner with me tonight.'

There was something about the way he issued the invitation that made her heart miss several beats. 'I really don't think I can,' she said hurriedly.

'Why not?'

'It's very kind of you…but I wouldn't want to intrude—'

'You're not intruding. I want you to stay.'

And the awful thing was that she wanted to stay, even though she knew she should be keeping her distance. 'Well, I suppose it would mean that we could do some more work later, after dinner.' She tried to justify the acceptance to herself.

'Are you for real?' Lucas fixed her with a teasing look.

The question and the way he looked at her made her skin flare with colour. 'Well...I'm just trying to be sensible. Time is imperative—'

'I think we will have done quite enough work by dinnertime,' he said firmly, and then pushed his chair back from the other side of the desk. 'Now, if you'll excuse me, I'll go through and see if Mrs Gordon will make us something to eat to tide us over until then.'

Penny sat back in her chair with a sigh as he left the room. If only he was cold and nasty this would be a lot easier. She glanced across to the other side of the desk and the files that he was working on and wondered if she should have a quick look through them before he got back. It would be just her luck if he found the papers. Then all this would be for nothing.

Hurriedly she got up and went around to try and scan through the remainder of his file. It would be a lot easier if she knew what the documents in question looked like, she thought.

Penny was leafing through a stack of letters when she came across some correspondence from her father that was dated last year. In excitement she started to delve deeper into the file. If there was one bit of information pertaining to her father in the box, then maybe the elusive documentation for his house would also be there.

She hadn't got very far when she heard Lucas's footsteps returning along the corridor outside.

Hastily Penny reached over and swapped his file with

the one she had been working on. Then returned to her seat.

'How's it going?' Lucas strode in just as she sat down.

'Fine.' She smiled up at him.

'Found anything?' He put a china mug of coffee down beside her.

'Not yet…'

'Maybe I'll be lucky with this file,' he said casually as he sat back down across the desk from her and reached for the box next to him. 'I noticed there was a few letters from William Kennedy in here, so maybe the documents for the house are here as well.'

'That does sound hopeful.' Penny could feel her stomach starting to tie into knots. She hadn't realised he'd already looked in the box. He was going to know that she had swapped them around!

'Strange…they don't seem to be here,' he murmured as he delved into the file.

'You mustn't be looking in the right box.' Penny got up and crossed to one of the filing cabinets behind him, busying herself putting away the papers she had already sorted. She couldn't bear to sit opposite him, because if he looked over at her directly and asked her if she had touched the file she was sure she would go bright red with guilt.

The door of the office opened and Mrs Gordon came in with some sandwiches. Isobel stood in the open doorway behind her.

'Daddy, you won't forget that you said you'd swim with me this afternoon,' she said shyly.

Lucas glanced over at his daughter and grinned. 'No, I won't forget, honey.'

The child smiled back and then ran into the office to climb up on his knee. 'How long will you be, Daddy?'

'Give me one hour and then I'll be all yours.' Lucas stroked her dark hair back from her face tenderly. 'Have you had some lunch?'

Isobel nodded. 'I had pizza.'

'Did you eat some salad with it?' Lucas asked with a raised eyebrow.

Isobel wrinkled her nose.

'You know you should eat something green, Issy...' Lucas said gently. 'We've talked about this be-fore...remember?'

'There is green jelly for afterwards,' the little girl said solemnly. 'I'm going to eat that.'

'That doesn't count.' Lucas tickled her and she giggled breathlessly. 'You'd better eat some salad, young lady, or you are going to be in big trouble.'

'Okay...okay...' The child squealed with laughter as he tickled her some more.

'Good girl.' He kissed her on the forehead. 'Now, run along and let Daddy get back to work. I'll see you for a swim a little later.'

The child wrapped her arms around his neck and kissed him back. 'I love you, Daddy.'

'I love you too.'

Isobel raced over to where Mrs Gordon was waiting for her by the door.

'Sorry about that,' Lucas said distractedly as he turned his attention back to his work. 'As you probably deduced, I'm going to have to leave you to it for a few hours and spend some time with my daughter.'

'That's okay.' Penny returned to her seat. The tender exchange between father and daughter had touched her. Lucas was obviously a devoted dad, and it made her like him even more. 'It must be difficult, running a business and being a single father.'

'It's not easy,' he admitted with a nod. 'And I hate it when I have to put in overtime. But Mrs Gordon is reliable, and Isobel adores her, so that takes a lot of the strain out of things.' He reached for the file in front of him.

Penny waited for him to comment again about the missing letters, but he said nothing further about them.

She glanced over at him. He was reading a document and seemed deep in thought. Uneasily she went back to the pile of papers in front of her. She didn't dare risk looking through the file with the letters in it, deciding that could wait until he'd left the room.

Silence descended between them, broken only by the rustling of paper and the occasional scribble of her pen as she labelled and reorganised.

'There's a stack of papers here that I think can be thrown away,' she murmured after a while. 'They seem to be mainly advertising bumph, but maybe you'd better look through them first, in case there is anything important there.'

'Fine—just put them to one side for me.' He barely looked up.

What was he so engrossed in? she wondered.

Silence resumed. Flint wandered in and sat down next to Lucas's chair. He leaned his head against his master's knee and Lucas stroked his head absently. The dog's breathing seemed loud, and the occasional thump of his tail on the polished floor distracted Penny.

'Well, that's all very interesting,' Lucas remarked suddenly.

'What is?'

'I've found some paperwork regarding the business partnership between my father and Kennedy.'

'Oh?'

'And I've found the deeds to the Kennedy property.' He held up some yellowing documents and smiled across at her.

Penny's eyes widened. She couldn't believe it; the damn papers had been in her file all along. If she hadn't swapped them over she would have found them. This was just her damn luck! 'Oh…great!' From somewhere she tried to insert enthusiasm into her voice. 'Does that mean you'll be able to proceed with the eviction straight away?'

'According to Salvador there are a few more papers I could do with—copies of earlier warning notices that have been sent to Kennedy, that kind of thing. But having the deeds strengthens my hand considerably.' Lucas pushed his chair back from the desk. 'I'll put them somewhere safe and take them to Salvador on Monday morning…or maybe tomorrow if he is free.'

Penny watched as he walked across and put them in the top drawer of a filing cabinet, then locked the file and put the key in his jeans pocket.

'I'm going to spend a little time with my daughter,' Lucas said easily. 'So, can I leave you to carry on sorting through the files and looking for those notices…?'

'Of course.' Her smile was somewhat strained.

She watched as he left the room, closely followed by Flint. Then she leaned back in her chair and groaned. If only she hadn't swapped that file…!

She supposed her only chance now was to find some of the other papers. Her eyes moved around the room, taking in the various boxes and metal cabinets. Suddenly her task seemed even more daunting than before. Apart from everything else, she had the horrible feeling that the real Mildred was going to turn up sooner than those papers were.

CHAPTER FOUR

PENNY worked solidly for the rest of the afternoon, but there was no sign of the missing papers. Her glance kept going over to the filing cabinet where the deeds to her father's house were. Knowing they were there and yet being unable to reach them was extremely frustrating. She wondered for the hundredth time why Lucas had locked them away.

The sound of a child's laughter drifted in from outside and Penny got up to look out of the window. She could just see the edge of a swimming pool and a long terrace, where a table and chairs were placed invitingly under the shade of a large parasol. As she watched Lucas swam into view, and then Isobel also appeared as she ran around the side of the pool dressed in a red swimming costume.

Lucas stood in the water and held his arms up for her. With a shriek of pleasure the child jumped in and then Lucas lifted her onto his shoulders.

'Again...again...' Her voice drifted in to Penny, as did her chuckles of delight as Lucas spun her around before helping her to get out so that the whole performance could be repeated.

He had infinite patience with her, Penny thought with a smile as she watched the game. Isobel clearly adored him. Water glistened on the powerful breadth of his shoulders and arms as he hoisted himself up out of the pool with athletic ease. And suddenly Penny found her mind drifting from how good a dad he was to what a fabulous body he had. His torso was strong and toned and incredibly powerful. She found herself wondering what it would feel like to be cradled in those arms... The very idea made her stomach muscles contract sharply with a thrust of pure desire.

Angrily she turned away from the window and returned to her work. She needed to stop thinking about Lucas in any other terms than those of the enemy. Anything else was pure folly. She was so annoyed with herself that it gave her the impetus to push on with even more speed through the next box of papers. But it didn't do her much good. The papers were nowhere in sight.

By the time Lucas returned to the office an hour later she had worked her way through several more boxes to no avail, and was feeling very dispirited.

'You've done well,' Lucas said with approval as he noticed the space she had cleared in the room. 'Any luck with those papers?'

She shook her head.

'Never mind. They are not so crucial now that I have the deeds. Maybe we'll find them tomorrow...' He smiled at her. 'In the meantime, why don't you join me in a pre-dinner drink out on the porch?'

Penny leaned back in her chair and looked up at him. He'd changed, she noticed, into black jeans and a black short-sleeved shirt. His hair was sleeked back from his face and was still damp from a shower.

It was a pity she found him so attractive, she thought hazily. It made the situation so much more perilous.

'What do you say?' He fixed her with a look that was slightly teasing. 'Shall we watch the sun go down over an ice-cold gin and tonic?'

The offer sounded incredibly tempting. Frankly, she'd had enough of being cooped up in here for one day.

Maybe a drink was just what she needed. 'That would be very nice.' Leaving her jacket hanging over the back of the chair, she stood up and followed him out of the office.

Although the air was warm outside there was a delicious breeze that soothed the senses. Penny leaned against the wooden rail of the veranda and stared out across the garden through the tracery of trees towards the sea. The sun was starting to go down in a brilliant blaze of blood orange that streaked the sky and lit the sea with incandescent splashes of fire.

Lucas joined her and handed across her drink.

'Thanks.' She smiled at him as she took it. 'You have a fabulous view from up here.'

'Yes, I do.'

For a moment there was silence as they both contemplated the sunset. She supposed she should have insisted on going back to her hotel, but it was very pleasant standing here with him. She turned slightly and looked over at him, only to find that his eyes were on her. Was it her imagination or was he watching her very closely?

'I suppose coming from Barbados you are used to stunning views?' he remarked.

It was a casual enough statement, yet it instantly set Penny on guard. 'Barbados is a beautiful island,' she agreed, her tone carefully neutral.

'Where did you used to live? The Caribbean side of the island or the Atlantic?'

'The Atlantic.' It wasn't a lie exactly; she had lived on the Atlantic coast of Arbuda.

'The views are spectacular there,' he said. 'Especially along the east coast road towards Bethsheba.'

'I take it you have visited Barbados?' She tried to change the slant of the conversation so that it was focused on him. These lies were making her far too uncomfortable.

'I go over on business a lot. But I also spent my honeymoon there.'

'That's a romantic place for a honeymoon,' she said softly.

'Yes...' Lucas paused for a moment, and Penny thought she glimpsed some raw emotion that was almost verging on anger in the darkness of his eyes, but it was hard to see him clearly. The sun was sinking fast now, and deep purple clouds of darkness were stealing over the landscape, shadows lengthening across the gardens and the porch.

'You must miss her a lot,' Penny said.

He inclined his head. 'It's been hard these last few years.'

Night dropped like a blanket over everything, and the sound of insects filled the heat of the air with a heavy cacophony.

'Do you mind my asking what happened to her? Or is that too personal a question?'

'No, I don't mind you asking.' He shrugged. 'She died trying to save a man from drowning. He shouldn't even have been in the water. Not only had he had too much to drink, but also they had issued storm warnings that day. The beach had red flags flying but he chose to ignore them. The really ironic thing was that the guy was okay. He managed to get back to shore, and Kay, who was a strong swimmer and taught physical education, didn't...'

Penny was horrified. 'Were you there when it happened?'

Lucas shook his head. 'No. I was at work. The first I

knew of it was when the police turned up at the office to give me the news.'

'I'm so sorry, Lucas. You must have been devastated.'

'It took me a while to come to terms with it, that's for sure.' Lucas took a sip of his drink. 'Anyway, that's enough of that depressing subject. Tell me about you.'

'Me? Well, there's not much to tell.' The swift change of subject caught her unawares.

'I don't believe that for one moment.' He grinned at her. 'I bet there are a lot of intriguing things you could tell me.'

'Depends what you call intriguing.' Penny was distinctly uncomfortable now.

'Well, for one thing how come your CV is less than accurate?'

'Is it?' Penny felt colour starting to seep into her face.

'You know it is. By all accounts, according to the paperwork the agency sent me, you should be fifty-five.' He grinned. 'How old are you anyway?'

'You know it's not gentlemanly to ask a lady her age,' Penny hedged.

'Well, I've never laid claim to being a gentleman,' he said with a spark of humour in his eye. 'I reckon you're twenty-six.'

'Twenty-eight,' she corrected him.

'So I rest my case. Something doesn't add up.'

'I've just found that employers tend to favour having an older woman as their PA, so I've used a little artistic licence on the forms, that's all.' She kept her voice airily light with intense difficulty. 'Once I'm in employment nobody has ever complained about my work.'

'And I'm not complaining either…at least not yet.' He grinned at her. 'So, apart from using artistic licence on forms, what else are you up to?'

'I beg your pardon?' Her heart bounced unevenly in her chest.

'What do you do in your spare time?' He clarified the question.

'Oh...I see.' She smiled and relaxed. 'Well, I like to read, listen to music, and do yoga for relaxation. And I learnt to sail when I lived in Ar...Barbados....' She trailed off in consternation. She had very nearly said Arbuda, had nearly blown her whole cover. Her heart raced against her chest. She was lousy at lying and she hated it. She especially hated lying to him—he seemed so...likeable.

His eyes flicked over her with a slow, assessing thoroughness. 'I like sailing too, when I get time. I have a yacht moored not far from here.'

At least he hadn't noticed her slip of the tongue, but she was going to have to be very careful.

'Maybe you'd like to accompany me one weekend?' he invited smoothly. 'As a thank-you for all your hard work.'

'That sounds wonderful.' She smiled. As she looked up into the darkness of his eyes she realised that it did indeed sound wonderful. She would have liked to spend more time with him. Get to know him better...

Hastily she looked away from him and sipped her drink. It wasn't going to happen. She was here for one reason only. He was her father's enemy and that was all she needed to know about him. Even thinking he was nice was a gross disloyalty.

'Maybe we could go next weekend,' he continued. 'I've got a feeling that we should have all this paperwork under control by then.'

'Let's hope so,' she said lightly.

'Well, if I haven't found the necessary papers by then

I may as well kiss goodbye to the whole Arbuda deal, because the planning permission runs out soon.' Lucas took a long swallow of his drink. 'Which means I'll probably lose my buyer for the project too.'

Penny looked up at him questioningly.

'A builder has offered me a good price for the Kennedy estate plus the beachfront land, and I have accepted it because I have no intention of developing the project myself. Only snag is that if we can't finalise by the end of this month the deal is off.'

'Shame.' Penny's voice was dry.

'Well, hopefully now I've found the deeds the other papers won't be far behind and we can get things moving.'

Not if I can help it, Penny thought glumly. The nerve of the guy! He had already found a buyer for her father's house and it didn't even belong to him yet! She wished for the millionth time that she had found the deeds first and buried them deep at the bottom of some drawer, where Lucas wouldn't find them for months. It would have served him right for heartlessly wanting to throw an old man out onto the streets.

The housekeeper came out of the doorway behind them. 'Dinner is served.'

'Thank you, Mrs Gordon.' Lucas smiled at Penny. 'Anyway, let's not talk any more about business for one night,' he said.

'No, let's not,' she agreed lightly. 'I think I'll be seeing business papers and box files in my dreams tonight.'

Lucas laughed. 'Sounds like a nightmare.'

In more ways than one, she thought as she followed him into the house.

The dining room was set with two places facing each other across the long table. Candlelight reflected and danced over the polished mahogany surface and silver cutlery. White lilies graced the sideboard next to them, scenting the room with their exotic fragrance.

'These are my favourite flowers,' Penny remarked as she stopped next to them to admire the display.

'Mrs Darien always liked the house to be filled with fresh flowers.' Mrs Gordon bustled past her to put some wine on the table. 'Lilies were her favourite too.'

'Mrs Gordon was devoted to my wife,' Lucas told Penny when they were left alone again. 'She looked after Kay when she was a little girl and she was the first person Kay thought of when we were looking for a house-keeper.'

Penny took her seat at the table. 'It must be a weight off your mind, knowing you have someone for Isobel that your wife approved of.'

'Yes, it is.'

'Daddy…' A small voice from the doorway made them both look round.

Isobel was standing just inside the room. She was dressed in a pair of white satin pyjamas, a teddy bear under her arm. 'Mrs Gordon says I've got to say good-night. But can't I stay up a bit longer…? There's no school tomorrow…'

'I don't think so, pumpkin, you've got an early start tomorrow… Grandma says she wants to pick you up at seven-thirty.'

Isobel padded further into the room. 'But I'm not tired.'

'You will be in the morning if you don't get a good night's sleep.' Lucas reached out an arm and lifted her up onto his knee. She giggled happily and looked across at Penny with wide, sparkling dark eyes.

'Are you Daddy's new girlfriend?'

For some reason the question made Penny self-consciously aware of Lucas's eyes resting on her. 'No, Isobel. I work for your daddy. I'm helping him tidy up all those files in the office.'

Isobel nodded. 'I'm going to be a fairy princess in the school play,' she told Penny seriously.

'I'm sure you will make a very beautiful fairy princess,' Penny said. 'What will you be wearing?'

Isobel frowned. 'I don't know.'

'Well, a fairy princess usually has a wand, with a star on the top, and sometimes she wears a crown on her head and has a long white dress. Do you think you'll be wearing something like that?'

'Maybe...' Isobel grinned, and Penny noticed she had a gap between her front teeth. 'Mrs Gordon is going to take me shopping.'

The housekeeper came in at that moment. 'I won't take you shopping if you aren't in bed in five minutes, young lady.'

Isobel squealed dramatically and then kissed her dad on the cheek. 'Night, Daddy.'

'Night, pumpkin. I'll be along soon to tuck you in.'

The child slipped down from his lap and then to Penny's surprise came around and reached up to kiss her goodnight as well. She smelt of baby lotion and talcum powder, and her hair was glossily soft next to Penny's skin for a moment before she drew back. 'Do you think I'll need wings to be a fairy princess?' she asked, looking up at her with intently serious eyes.

'Most definitely,' Penny said solemnly. 'All fairy princess have wings.'

Isobel smiled. 'I can't wait,' she said happily. Then with a little wave in her father's direction she left the room.

'She's been talking about nothing but this school play for the last week,' Mrs Gordon said with an amused smile as she put their appetisers on the table in front of them. 'I think maybe she's going to go on the stage when she grows up. She's a real little actress.'

'Adorable with it,' Penny said instantly.

'Yes, she is.' The housekeeper smiled at her. 'Anyway, I'll leave you to enjoy your meal.'

As the woman left the room Lucas reached to pour some wine in Penny's glass. 'How are you finding things at the hotel, Mildred?' he asked casually.

'It's very comfortable.' She still found it strange answering to that name.

'I suppose you'll be looking around for an apartment soon? That's if you decide to stay on here, of course.'

'I suppose so. I haven't really thought about it yet.' She pretended to be interested in the prawn and avocado starter before her. 'This looks delicious,' she said, hoping to change the subject away from her plans for the future.

'Yes, Mrs Gordon is very skilled in the kitchen,' Lucas agreed, before continuing right back with the conversation. 'There are some new apartment buildings not far from the office, and I've heard good reports about them. Apparently they're well designed. It wouldn't hurt to go and look at them.'

'I'll bear that in mind, Lucas,' she said off-handedly.

'They are rental apartments, so it wouldn't be too big a commitment.' He smiled at her. 'Bearing in mind that you're a free spirit.'

She reached for her wine and took a sip. 'Maybe I'll go and take a look next week...if I've got time.'

'I'll give you an extra long lunch on Monday.'

'Are you on commission for these apartments?' she

asked him, her eyes sparkling with amusement. 'You seem very keen for me to look at them.'

'Just trying to be helpful,' he said easily. 'I know it must be difficult for you, settling in to a new job and looking for somewhere to live all at the same time. I think looking around at the accommodation available will give you a better idea of whether you want to stay on here or not.'

His thoughtfulness touched her, made her wish for a moment that she really was intending to stay on as his PA. 'Thanks, Lucas, I appreciate that.' She felt so guilty that she couldn't quite meet his eye as she spoke.

Penny was glad when Mrs Gordon bustled in to clear the table.

'If you'll excuse me for a moment, Mildred.' Lucas pushed his chair back from the table. 'I'll just go tuck Isobel in and wish her goodnight.'

'Yes, of course.' For a little while Penny was left alone in the room. She toyed with her wine glass, watching the way the candlelight twinkled over the crystal. Her surroundings were so tranquil that it added to the sense of unreality inside her. She shouldn't be here; she shouldn't be doing this, a small voice told her sharply.

Maybe she should leave now, just walk away while there was no real harm done. She had merely helped Lucas to tidy his office. Even if she wasn't the real Mildred, how annoyed could he be about a little unpaid clerical assistance when he was so clearly desperate for staff?

As she made to push her chair away from the table Mrs Gordon came back into the room with their main course. 'There you are, dear,' she said, as she placed a plate in front of her with succulent slices of roast beef on it. 'Lucas will be along in a moment; Isobel is always asleep within two minutes once he's tucked her up.'

'Thank you.' Penny smiled at the woman and realised that walking out wasn't really an option. It would be incredibly rude after Mrs Gordon had gone to so much trouble. Maybe she should feign illness once Lucas got back to the table? She could have a sudden migraine attack and get him to drop her back at the hotel. At least once she was there she could think a little more clearly about all this. Sitting here accepting Lucas's hospitality just didn't feel right.

The housekeeper put down a serving dish of potatoes and vegetables. 'If you don't mind my saying so, you remind me somewhat of Lucas's late wife,' she said suddenly as she glanced across at her. 'Kay had the same beautiful blonde hair and green eyes.'

'Did she?' Penny was taken aback by the observation. 'Isobel has such dark hair I would have thought Kay would have been dark also.'

Mrs Gordon shook her head. 'Isobel is like her father; she has his Spanish blood. And of course Lucas takes after his mother...Isabella. She was a most beautiful woman.'

'Getting the family history, I hear,' Lucas said with a grin as he returned to the room.

'I'm just saying how beautiful your mother was,' Mrs Gordon continued unabashed. 'How is Isobel?'

'Fast asleep, thanks, Mrs Gordon.'

With a satisfied nod the housekeeper left the room.

'Mrs Gordon could sit an exam on my family and pass with honours,' Lucas said with a grin as the door closed behind her.

The woman was certainly right about one thing, Penny

thought as she glanced across at him. Lucas looked nothing like his father…and maybe he was nothing like him in character either.

'Would you like more wine?' Lucas asked, and lifted the bottle towards her glass.

'No, thank you.' Hurriedly she declined, and noticed that he put the bottle down without refilling his own glass.

'I'll keep a clear head for later,' he said when he caught her eye.

'Later?' She wondered if it was her imagination—or did his voice hold the husky promise of invitation…?

'Driving you home.'

'Oh, I see.' For some reason she found herself blushing. 'I can take a taxi, Lucas.'

'I wouldn't hear of it.' Lucas waved the offer aside dismissively. 'I'd like to see you home.' There was a certain warmth about his tone and in his eyes that sent little darts of awareness rushing through her.

'So tell me a little more about yourself…Milly. May I call you Milly? It seems somehow to suit you more than Mildred.'

'Does it?' She moistened her lips nervously.

'Yes, it does.' He smiled.

Their eyes met and held across the table and she felt her heart give a crazy kind of skip.

She wondered what would happen if she told him the truth right now. Would he hate her and throw her out without waiting for an explanation? Or would he patiently listen to what she had to say?

The thought of him hating her was appalling.

'Tell me what it was like growing up in Barbados,' Lucas invited lazily.

Hastily she pulled herself together. 'Much the same as growing up here, I would imagine.'

'I went to boarding school in England for a good many years,' Lucas said. 'It was the place my father was educated and he was determined I should go there as well. So I suppose you could say that I grew up in England.'

'Were you homesick?' Penny asked curiously.

'I got used to it.' He shrugged. 'My mother, however, was never happy about it. But my father was a forceful character; he usually got his own way.'

'I can imagine,' Penny muttered with icy disdain, then noticed Lucas looking at her quizzically and realised she had probably sounded too vehement. 'I mean...I can imagine it was difficult for your mother. She must have missed you.' Quickly she tried to soften her tone.

'Yes, I suppose she did. I was an only child, and my father was away a lot on business.'

Yes, he was in Arbuda, having an affair, Penny thought disdainfully. She felt sorry for Lucas's mother. Not only had her husband been an overbearing tyrant but he had been unfaithful to her as well. She wondered if Isabella had known.

'I take it from what Mrs Gordon was saying that your mother is dead now?'

Lucas nodded. 'She died twelve years ago.'

'I'm sorry.' She wondered if Lucas had any idea about what had really gone on in Arbuda.

'And did you get on with your father?' she asked him curiously.

'We had our disagreements...' He shrugged. 'But thankfully we patched up our differences before he died. I'm glad of that.'

Which meant that he probably wouldn't want to hear

anything negative about his father now, Penny thought dryly.

'What about you?' Lucas asked. 'Did you have a good relationship with your parents?'

'Very. But my mother died when I was sixteen and Dad was low for a while after that. Unfortunately he made some bad decisions around that time. Got involved in a business deal with a very dodgy character…a man who had a hidden agenda…and from having a nice comfortable home things started to go downhill. I did what I could to help him, took over the running of the house and tried very hard to sort things out, but it was a difficult situation and it went from bad to worse.'

'So how is your father now?' Lucas asked.

'Financially he never recovered…' Penny hesitated. 'But he is still battling on and I'm hoping things will improve for him soon.'

'It sounds like he's had a tough time.' Lucas sounded sympathetic.

'Yes, and all because he was taken in by a confidence trickster.' Penny's eyes shimmered.

'Have you tried to redress the situation by law?'

'Oh, yes. Solicitors' letters have been flying backwards and forwards for years. All that happens is that the bills grow bigger. The debt piles up.'

'Maybe it's time he just cut his losses?' Lucas said quietly.

'I think he'd rather die than do that…'

'It's only money—and at least he has a loving and supportive daughter. That means a lot.'

A loving and supportive daughter who was dining with the enemy, Penny thought guiltily. And, what was worse, she was enjoying dining with the enemy. He seemed very easy to talk to, very charming. But then her mother had probably thought that about Lawrence Darien.

Outside in the hall the grandfather clock struck ten, the chimes echoing in the stillness of the house.

There was really no point sitting here telling Lucas about her father unless she told him the whole truth...and if she did that all hell might break loose. Speaking ill of the dead was a risky business, even under ordinary circumstances. And these were certainly not ordinary circumstances. She should have made her excuses and left ages ago, as she had planned.

'That was a delicious dinner, but I really should be going.' She straightened her cutlery on the plate.

'So soon?' He frowned. 'At least have coffee with me in the lounge first.'

Penny shook her head and got hastily to her feet. 'I'd better not. I didn't realise it was so late.'

'You must be tired.' Lucas also stood up, and walked around towards her. 'Don't worry about starting too early in the morning. Now that I've found those deeds some of the pressure is off. I might drop them over to Salvador's house in the morning. That way I could pick you up about eleven, if that's all right?'

'Fine.' The mention of those deeds made her tense up inside.

'And don't worry too much about your father, Milly,' he said softly. 'I know it's an old cliché, but if he has his health, really, at the end of the day, that is the most important thing.'

'You think so?' For some reason his matter-of-fact statement made her angry, especially as it was spoken in almost the same breath as his mentioning the deeds of her father's house.

It was easy for him to be so laid back, but what would

he say if it was his father in this situation? If it was his father who was going through hell? 'But money is important, Lucas,' she said with brittle emphasis. 'Let's face it, if it wasn't you wouldn't be getting ready to evict some old man from his home.'

For a second Lucas's eyes narrowed on her face. 'That's totally different.'

'I can't see that it is.' Her voice trembled slightly.

'Hey…' Lucas reached out and much to her consternation put a hand under her chin, tipping her face up towards his. 'Are you okay?'

'Of course I am.' She swallowed hard.

'This business in Arbuda is part of my father's last will and testament. He has requested specifically that I follow it through…' Lucas trailed off. 'Anyway, Salvador is looking in to all that for me. I assure you everything is being done decently.'

'Is it?' Penny was distracted suddenly as his hand seemed to trail upwards over her face in a butterfly caress.

And suddenly she wasn't thinking about her father any more. Instead her eyes were locked with his and she could feel small shivers of awareness shooting through her. She felt suddenly breathless with a strange kind of excitement…the kind that made her body tingle and her pulses quicken. His hand traced lightly across her cheekbones, setting her skin on fire, and then trailed through the soft silkiness of her hair.

Penny felt a thrill shooting through her that was so intense it was shocking, and there was a strange magnetic intensity between her body and his. He was standing only a few inches away, and yet she could feel the pull of his body inviting her closer. She wanted to move into his arms so badly that it was a physical effort not to sway closer.

His gaze moved to the softness of her mouth and she imagined she could almost feel his eyes touching her. She moistened her lips nervously as they tingled with the anticipation and the need for him to kiss her.

'Milly…' He breathed her name in an undertone.

Except it wasn't her name…she was here under false pretences. The fact flicked through her mind with lightning speed. She needed to back away from this quickly. Yet she couldn't seem to make herself. Her brain was logically telling her one thing but her body was saying something quite different, and with much more force.

Then, quite unexpectedly, Lucas was the one to step back. Penny wondered if she had misread the signs, if the chemistry that had flared between them had been all in her mind. She looked up at him wordlessly, and in the ensuing silence she could hear her heart hammering fiercely against her chest.

'Milly, I—' Whatever he had been about to say was interrupted by an almighty clatter coming from outside the room. 'What on earth was that?' he muttered in consternation, and hurried out to investigate.

Penny followed him into the hallway. There was the sound of someone moaning in pain and they quickly followed the noise down and into the kitchen. Mrs Gordon was lying on the kitchen floor, her leg twisted at an awkward angle beneath her, cutlery and pots and pans on the tiled floor around her.

'My God, are you all right?' Lucas was instantly beside her, his tone laced with deep concern.

'Yes…yes, I'm okay.' The woman moved and managed to sit up, but her face was white and her lips quivered as if she might burst into tears at any moment. 'What a mess,' she wailed as she looked around her at the floor. 'I tried to catch hold of the table to break my fall and everything came tumbling down on top of me.'

'Never mind the mess,' Lucas said impatiently. 'The most important thing is you. Do you think you've broken anything?'

'No.' The housekeeper moved her foot and winced. 'I can't believe I was so stupid. I spilt some water on the floor and forgot to mop it up immediately. Then the next thing I knew my legs just went beneath me... So silly...I'm always telling Isobel to be careful when these tiles are wet.' She flinched as she tried to get up.

'Maybe you'd better not move,' Lucas said gently. 'Where does it hurt?'

'I'll be all right.' With grim determination Mrs Gordon tried to hoist herself up, using the edge of the table.

'Okay...if you must get up, let me help you.' Hurriedly Lucas put an arm around her and lifted her to her feet.

'Thank you.' She smiled bravely as she leaned against the table. 'See—I'm fine.' But as soon as she put her foot down on the ground her face crumpled in agony.

'We should ring for an ambulance,' Lucas said firmly.

'No!' The woman looked horrified. 'I don't want all that fuss.'

'You need to get to hospital, Mrs Gordon,' Penny said gently.

'I'll be fine...really.' Even as she was speaking she was trying to gingerly test her foot on the floor again. But she was obviously in excruciating pain.

'I'll take you down to Casualty myself,' Lucas said determinedly. 'You've got to go and get checked out.' As he spoke Lucas moved to pick up a set of keys that were hanging by the back door. 'Will you keep an eye on Isobel for me while I'm gone?' He looked around at Penny and she nodded her head.

'Of course I will.'

'Thanks.' He smiled at her and then, ignoring his housekeeper's protests, scooped her up as if she were a mere lightweight and carried her towards the door.

Penny hurried to open it for him, and then followed them out through the night to open the passenger door of his car for them as well.

'All this fuss over a small fall,' Mrs Gordon said, her voice breaking on a sob. 'I'll be all right after a good night's sleep.'

'I'll feel better if you are properly checked over,' Lucas said soothingly. 'Please don't fret, Ethel.' Gently he tucked her skirt inside the car so that the door wouldn't catch it.

'We'll be back as soon as possible, Milly,' he said as he strode around to get into the car himself.

'That's okay. There's no hurry.' Penny stepped back and watched as he started the engine and the car pulled away down the driveway. Only when the lights had faded into the darkness did she return to the house.

CHAPTER FIVE

PENNY wandered back through the hallway and stood listening for any sound from Isobel. But all she could hear was the gentle rhythmic tick of the clock. Obviously the child was still fast asleep. She glanced through the doorway into the dining room, noting the dishes waiting to be cleared from the table. It seemed sensible to start tidying up. At least it would be one less worry for Lucas and Mrs Gordon when they returned from the hospital.

It didn't take long to clear the dining room, and then Penny started on the kitchen, lifting the debris from the floor and stacking the dishwasher before mopping and drying the tiles so that there would be no more accidents. The kitchen was a dream to work in. Every modern convenience was stowed away behind the shiny white units, and it was good to keep busy; it took her mind away from thinking about Lucas and the desire that had flared as soon as he had touched her. He seemed to have a strange power over her senses, a power that was extremely disconcerting.

She remembered how lovely he had been with Mrs Gordon, so gentle and concerned, and even that made her insides turn to gooey emotion. Ferociously she scrubbed at the kitchen counters until they gleamed. She wouldn't give those thoughts any space, she told herself angrily. Instead she would dwell on why she was here...and also poor Mrs Gordon. The woman had looked extremely shaken by that fall; she hoped that she hadn't broken anything.

The kitchen done, Penny meandered back into the hall. It seemed strange being alone in this house. She supposed she really should be making the most of the situation by going into the office and searching for those papers, but somehow it seemed a little too underhanded when Lucas was at a hospital on a mission of mercy.

On the other hand, the sooner she found those papers the sooner she could put all this behind her and get on with her own life. Penny paused by the door to the office. She had just reached out and turned the handle when a shrill ringing filled the silence. For a moment she imagined it was an alarm, then she realised that it was the phone. With a wry grin at her foolish imagination she hurried inside to answer it.

'Hi, it's me.' Lucas's voice sounded velvety-warm down the phone.

'Hi, how's Mrs Gordon?'

'Well, the good news is that she hasn't broken her ankle. The bad news is that there is a problem with her hip and they want to keep her in for observation.'

'Oh, no! The poor woman.'

'Yes, she's totally spooked. Hates hospitals. Anyway, I've rung her sister and she's on her way. But I think I'd better hang around until she arrives.'

'That's okay, Lucas. I'll just wait for you.'

'The thing is I might not be home for another couple of hours, and you must be exhausted. I was thinking it might be sensible if you bunk down in the spare bedroom. It's already made up.'

'I'm not that tired, Lucas,' she said quickly. 'I can wait up for you.'

'But then you'll have to get a taxi back to the hotel because I can't leave Isobel alone,' Lucas said calmly. 'Take the spare bedroom; it's the last door on the right upstairs. At least that way you'll get some sleep. Just make yourself at home.'

The phone went dead before she could argue further. Penny sat down on the edge of the office desk and glanced over at the filing cabinets. By the sounds of things she had a good few hours to go through them.

She stood up and opened the first drawer. *Make yourself at home…* Lucas's words echoed in her mind as she stared down at the papers inside. They had a warm ring to them and from nowhere she felt a fierce thrust of guilt.

'Damn it all,' she muttered vehemently, and slammed the drawer shut again. Then she turned and left the room. Somehow she didn't have the heart to go rummaging through files now.

Having these attacks of conscience wasn't helping her father, she told herself angrily as she went upstairs. She would have to get on with searching for those papers first thing tomorrow. It was either that or leave.

She paused by an open door halfway along the landing. It was Isobel's room. A small night lamp was on, highlighting the soft pink walls and the pink and white patchwork quilt that covered the bed. Penny crept in to check on the little girl. She was fast asleep, the covers thrown back slightly. Penny tucked them in around her and, noticing her teddy bear had slipped down between the bed and the side table, placed it in next to her again.

Poor little mite, she thought, watching over her for a moment. It couldn't be easy growing up without her mum. Quietly she slipped back out into the corridor.

The room next door was obviously Mrs Gordon's, judging by the voluminous purple dress hanging on the side of the wardrobe.

Lucas's room was across from that. She knew it was his room because it was so typically masculine. There was an enormous bed, with a pale grey cover on it, a computer in one corner with a stack of books sitting next to it, and a trouser press with a pair of jeans hanging over it.

She walked further on and opened the door at the end of the corridor. It was decorated in shades of lilac and white, with white wicker furniture, and had a country-fresh feel about it. The bed looked extremely inviting. Maybe she would take up Lucas's offer and bunk down for the night. At least that way she could get up early in the morning and get on with looking through those files. Closing the door behind her, she stripped off and slipped beneath the cool sheets.

As soon as her head hit the pillow she was asleep.

Her dreams that night were as troubled as her thoughts had been by day. One moment she was telling Lucas the truth...the next she was creeping out of the house, the deeds to her father's house tucked into her handbag. Stealing the papers had never been her intention, and she woke up in a cold panic, her heart thudding with fear.

The room was in pitch darkness, and for a few moments she couldn't remember where she was. There was a strange sound in the darkness, like a distant wailing. It took a moment for her to remember that she was at Lucas's house and that the noise was probably Isobel crying. Swiftly she threw back the covers, pulled on her trousers, buttoned up her top and hurried along to the child's room.

The little girl was sitting on the edge of her bed, sobbing uncontrollably.

'What's the matter, darling?' Penny said soothingly as she went across to her.

'Want my daddy.'

'Daddy will be here soon. He had to take Mrs Gordon

to the doctor because she had a sore leg.' Penny sat down beside her and put an arm around her. 'But it's nothing to worry about.'

Isobel looked up at her, her eyes brimming with tears. 'Why does Mrs Gordon have a sore leg?'

'Because she slipped on the kitchen floor.' Penny pulled back the bed covers. 'But she'll be better soon, and Daddy will be home. Now, why don't you get back into bed and try and get some sleep? You're going out with your grandma in the morning, aren't you?'

Isobel nodded, but made no move to get into the bed. 'Will Mrs Gordon have to go to heaven, like Mummy?' A huge tear spilled down her cheek.

'Oh, no, darling.' Penny's heart went out to the little girl and she wrapped her arms around her and held her tight. 'Mrs Gordon will be just fine.'

'Promise?' Isobel looked up at her, and when Penny nodded she snuggled happily back into her arms. Penny stroked the dark hair soothingly and rocked her for a few moments. It felt strangely comforting, holding the warmth of the child close in her arms.

'Now, let's have no more tears,' she whispered. 'There's nothing to be scared about.'

'There might be a bogeyman under the bed,' Isobel murmured solemnly. 'I'd be scared of that.'

'There's no such thing as bogeymen.'

'Sure?' Isobel looked up at her again with big wide eyes.

Penny grinned. 'I'm positive.'

Isobel cuddled in against her again.

'You really should be getting back to sleep. It must be very late...' Penny glanced up as a movement in the doorway caught her eye. Lucas was standing there watching them. He smiled at Penny as their eyes met.

'How long have you been there?' she asked in surprise.

'A few minutes. I've just got back from the hospital.'

Isobel looked up as she heard her father's voice. 'Daddy!' she squealed with delight, and flung herself off the bed to go and run into his arms.

'You should be in bed and asleep, young lady. It's three in the morning,' he said as he swung her up into his arms.

'I had a bad dream and I woke up. I thought there was a bogeyman under the bed.'

'As Milly said, there's no such thing as bogeymen,' Lucas told her gently. 'So back to bed with you.'

Penny moved out of the way as he carried the child back to her bed. She watched as he tucked her up.

'Sweet dreams, pumpkin,' he said.

'Night, Daddy,' Isobel snuggled down contentedly. 'Night, Milly.'

'Night, sweetheart.' Penny smiled.

Isobel looked as if she was fighting to keep her eyes open as they turned and left the room.

'So how is Mrs Gordon?' Penny asked as soon as they were out of earshot.

'Not good.' Lucas pulled the door closed behind them. 'Apparently she has been having a lot of pain in her hip for the last few months. But she's been too scared to go and see a doctor. This fall has just aggravated the problem further.'

'Poor woman.' Penny's face creased in concern. 'What do they think is wrong?'

'One of the doctors said it looked from the X-ray as if there was a problem with the hip joint which could have been caused by arthritis.' Lucas shrugged. 'But we'll know more tomorrow, when the consultant sees her.'

His eyes flicked down over her body. 'Did you get dressed in a hurry?' he asked with a grin.

She followed his eyes down and noticed her top was buttoned crookedly. Suddenly she was extremely conscious of her untidy appearance. Her blonde hair was tousled and loose around her shoulders, she was wearing no make-up and her clothes weren't even on correctly. 'I must look a mess...' Hurriedly she tried to rebutton her top. 'I was in bed asleep when I heard Isobel crying.'

'I don't think you could ever look a mess, Milly,' he said huskily. 'On the contrary, you are a very beautiful woman.'

The compliment and the way he was looking at her made her temperature suddenly shoot up. 'Thank you...I wasn't fishing for compliments.'

'I know that.' He noted that she was buttoning her top up crookedly again. 'Do you want a hand with that?' There was a hint of dry amusement in the darkness of his eyes.

'No, thank you.' She dropped her hands to her sides; they were far too unsteady to sort the problem out now. 'Anyway, it's late...I suppose we should turn in.'

'I suppose we should.'

He made no attempt to move away and neither did she; they just stood there looking at each other. To her consternation she could feel an intimate sense of awareness spiralling between them, just as it had earlier.

'Thanks for looking after Isobel for me tonight. You were great with her,' he said softly.

'It wasn't difficult. She's a lovely child.' She swallowed hard and tried to wrench her eyes away from the mesmerising force of his, but she couldn't. 'Anyway...you must be tired; it's been a long day.' She tried again to be strong and sensible and move away. The words sounded good, yet her body refused to put them into action.

'I'm not in the slightest bit tired,' he murmured. He reached out and smoothed a stray strand of her hair away from her face. The gentle touch of his hand against her skin sent a shivery erotic sensation flooding through her.

'Neither am I,' she whispered shakily.

'I know…' His eyes raked over her face, lingering on her lips. 'There is a certain chemistry between us…isn't there?'

It was more of a statement than a question, so she made no reply.

'And I've been wondering what to do about it ever since we were interrupted at this point earlier today.'

'Have you…?' She found herself swaying a little closer. What would it be like to kiss him? she wondered. Her heart thundered in her ears as if she had been running.

'And I've wondered how politically correct it would be to do this…' He bent closer and his lips connected with hers in a butterfly caress that set off an explosion of passionate sensation inside her. 'I keep trying to convince myself that this isn't a good idea,' he murmured, and he pulled back fractionally, his eyes on her lips, his breath soft against her skin. 'I keep telling myself that you work for me, and mixing business with pleasure can cause all kinds of complications…' As he spoke he brushed his lips lightly against hers again, in a feather-light provocative way that made her ache for so much more.

'You're right…' she murmured unsteadily. 'All kinds of complications…' And in more ways than one, she added silently, trying to make herself pull back from the situation. She was here under false pretences, for a start, so an affair of the heart was out of the question, and as she had never been a person who indulged in casual sex, it was time to move away now. Her mind registered the command but still she didn't move. She felt spellbound by his closeness.

'But then I thought…what the hell…?' As Lucas was speaking he traced the line of her mouth with one forefinger, sending shivery sensations of pure hunger racing through her. 'Maybe this is a risk worth taking…'

The rasping deep tones of his voice seemed to inflame her senses even more. 'Maybe it is…' she found herself agreeing softly.

He moved even closer then, lacing both hands through the softness of her hair, and held her in a possessive way as he kissed her again. Her resistance to him crumbled totally and this time she kissed him back, fire racing through her veins, adrenalin pumping. The kiss deepened and suddenly nothing mattered except the urgent demands of her body.

Penny wasn't even able to think straight any more. Everything was just a wild blur of complete and utter longing.

She felt his hands caressing up over her body, finding the aroused hard thrust of her naked breast through the cotton material of her blouse. The sensation of his fingers teasing her erect nipple through the light clothing was unbearably erotic. His tongue invaded the softness of her mouth, his kisses becoming more and more heated and demanding.

She stood on tiptoe, responding to him with equal passion, pressing closer against him.

'I've been wondering what this would feel like since the first moment you walked into my office,' he murmured.

'So have I,' she admitted shakily.

He smiled, and then, taking hold of her hand, he led her into his bedroom.

Penny's heart was thundering so heavily against her chest that it was like a wild animal trying to escape. The rational side of her brain told her that this was a mistake. But the voice of reason was a mere whisper against the hurricane force of her need for him.

He turned on the bedside lamp and it threw the room into a shadowy gold light.

Penny watched as he tore off his shirt. She noticed the way his muscles rippled with strength and vitality under the honey bronze of his skin, and she felt her stomach muscles contract into sharp knots of desire. She sat down on the edge of the bed, wondering if this was all a dream... Maybe she hadn't really woken up?

He reached for the buckle on his trousers and unfastened it. She had never really thought that a man's body was beautiful before...but his was. It was sheer perfection. From the broad, powerful shoulders to the narrow hips, he had the sort of body that could have belonged to an athlete, honed and tuned and in the peak of physical condition.

He glanced over at her, caught her watching him and grinned. Then he approached the bed, with a look of purpose in the dark eyes that made her heart beat even faster.

'Lucas, are we doing the right thing...?' she murmured, a note of panic in her voice.

He smiled and then reached out and unbuttoned her blouse, revealing the upward tilt of her breasts, the erect nipples. 'Your body seems to think so...and so does mine.'

As if to prove the point his fingers moved over her womanly curves and she closed her eyes as a burning wave of pleasure shot through her. She leaned back against the satin covers of the bed and helped him to remove the rest of her clothing, her fingers as frantic and feverish for him as his were for her.

CHAPTER SIX

WHEN Penny woke up the room was lit by a shadowy silver light cast from the outside landing. At some point Lucas must have switched off the bedside lamp, but Penny didn't remember that. All she remembered was the wild passion, the heat of his kisses, and the feel of his hands as they took her to heights she had never reached before. No one had ever made her feel like that before...not even Nick, and she had been deeply in love with him. The knowledge was deeply perturbing. Last night had been a mistake. Lucas Darien was the enemy.

She turned her head and looked across at him. He was fast asleep, lying on his side facing her. The covers had slipped from his shoulders, revealing the power of his body. Just looking at him made her stomach dip, as if she was on a swing and someone had pushed her too high, too hard. Her eyes drifted over the contours of his face, taking the opportunity to study him in sleep. His features were classically perfect: a strong, chiselled jawline, high cheekbones and a wide forehead. She noticed the length of his dark lashes, the sensual, soft curve of his mouth. And suddenly she wanted to reach out and touch him, cuddle into the protective curve of those arms, press her lips against his. She didn't want Lucas to be the enemy...she really didn't.

As if he sensed her watching him, he suddenly opened his eyes and their gaze connected.

He smiled lazily at her and her heart dipped with longing. 'Good morning.'

'Morning,' she murmured, thinking how formal and polite they sounded after a night of such intimacy.

'What time is it?'

'I don't know.' Trying to keep the covers over her nakedness, she stretched out her arm to peer at her watch. 'Five-thirty…I think.'

'Plenty of time, then.'

'Plenty of time for what?'

He gave a low laugh and rolled over so that he was pinning her against the mattress. 'What do you think?' he murmured playfully.

The sudden contact of his body against hers made her insides dissolve in longing. Then he kissed her, a long, lingering, warm kiss that sent her senses reeling into further chaos.

The feelings inside her were intensely conflicting. One part of her was telling her that this was wrong…that she was losing sight of the truth and her real reason for being here. The other part of her was recklessly trying to ignore all those warnings because she wanted him so much. It was a whole new experience for Penny; she had never had to fight with herself like this before—she had always been perfectly in control of her emotions.

'Being here with you like this is probably a big mistake,' she whispered, but at the same time she was running her fingers through the soft darkness of his hair almost wondrously, loving the texture of it against her hands, loving the freedom of being able to stroke him, touch him.

'Why is that?' he asked lazily, peppering her forehead and her cheeks and then the sides of her throat with kisses.

She hadn't even realised she had spoken aloud until he asked. 'I suppose for the same reasons you were expounding last night.' She murmured the excuse almost off-handedly, not wanting to think too deeply about anything except what he was doing to her.

Maybe it was the strange half-light of the room, or just the closeness of his naked body, but she had totally lost all inhibitions. She arched her back as his lips moved lower down to the hollow of her chest. Her body was clamouring wildly for him to touch her more intimately. She ached to feel his mouth against her breasts.

'Mmm…but after last night I think those worries have evaporated… What we shared was far too pleasurable to ever be classed as a mistake…' His hands travelled up over the curve of her hips, smoothing into her waist and then higher.

'Definitely,' she murmured breathlessly as his fingers moved over her breast, closing over the rosy hard peak of her desire. 'After all…' She gasped a little as his mouth followed the path of his hands. 'This is just sex—' She broke off as he pulled away from her slightly. 'What's the matter?' she asked throatily.

His dark eyes locked with hers in amusement. 'Nothing…I just didn't realise you were so modern in your approach to lovemaking.'

She felt herself colouring up with a different kind of heat now. The ironic thing was that she was anything but modern in her approach to lovemaking…she had never indulged in a one-night stand before in her life, had always needed to feel deeply involved with a man before going to bed with him. But she was enough of a realist to know that kind of a relationship was out of the question between them.

How could this ever be anything other than just a casual liaison when she had told him so many lies? And apart from that he was the one man in the world she should definitely not have taken to bed. She was betraying her father with every minute she was in his arms. She was sleeping with the enemy. The hard, cold facts thumped through her mind in unrelenting waves of condemnation.

There would never be a future for them as a couple.

'I just meant that there need be no recriminations between us tomorrow…' she murmured shakily, trying not to care too deeply. If all she could have of him was now then she would take what she could.

'Definitely no recriminations,' he agreed. His eyes moved over her heated countenance, taking in the vulnerable light in her green-gold eyes and the soft curve of her lips. He stroked his hand soothingly across her cheekbones, feeling the heat of her skin, and then threaded his hands through the silky cloud of her hair that was spread across the pillows around her. 'I learnt long ago not to worry about what might happen in the future…now is all that matters.'

'And this is just a bit of fun. Why shouldn't we enjoy ourselves…?' she whispered as his lips trailed up the column of her neck to the sensitive hollow of her throat.

'Why not, indeed?' he agreed lazily, moving further up to nibble on her ear.

Desperately she was trying to formulate sensible thoughts, whilst at the same time her body was driving her to new heights of need.

He found her lips and kissed her in a slow, intense way that drugged her senses even more. Then he pulled her closer and their bodies merged as one in a powerful, intoxicating rhythm.

Lucas was a masterful lover, totally skilled at turning a woman on, and she revelled in the warmth and passion of his body, meeting fire with fire. As she drowned in the heady experience the real world seemed to blur into insignificance. Nothing else mattered except here and now. Again and again he brought her to the brink of ecstasy, controlling her, playing with her until she was almost begging for release and total fulfilment. Then, just when she thought she couldn't wait any longer, he tipped her over the edge onto a rollercoaster of thunderous, joyful fulfilment.

She clung to him breathlessly afterwards. Neither of them spoke. There seemed no need for words; the way he cradled her close and stroked her hair seemed words enough.

Contentedly she drifted to sleep, secure in the powerful circle of his arms.

When Penny next opened her eyes, she felt warm and lazily content; she reached out across the bed, searching for Lucas, wanting to snuggle back into his arms, but her hands found only the cool empty space in the bed next to her. She sat up, brushing the weight of her hair back from her face as she glanced around. 'Lucas?'

There was no reply. She was alone in the room. Penny lay back against the pillows and looked at her watch. It was almost nine-thirty! She couldn't believe she had slept so late. Or maybe she could after the activity of the night… Her lips curved in a smile. Lucas had been the most incredible lover. Just thinking about what he had done to her made her insides melt all over again…made her want to do it all over again.

Sunlight was creeping into the room through a chink in the curtains. She watched the way it played over the satin bedcovers and felt warm and dreamy. She wished Lucas was here with her now—in fact she wished that every night could be spent like last night, wrapped in his arms…

Suddenly her thoughts froze as a swift surge of reality brutally attacked the wistful feelings inside her. She was being crazy. Sleeping with Lucas had been a one-off event. It could never happen again. Okay, last night had been wildly exciting and deeply satisfying, but it had also been incredibly reckless. She was here to help her father and there was no escaping that fact. And, what was more, if she didn't hurry and get out of here she would be exposed as a fraud by the real Mildred Bancroft—and she was damned sure Lucas wouldn't want to take her into his arms when that happened. He'd be livid and she couldn't honestly blame him.

Angry with herself for caring, she swung her legs out of bed and headed for the *en suite* bathroom. Her first loyalty had to be to her father.

What she needed to do today was find those papers, put them somewhere Lucas wouldn't think of looking for them, and then leave post haste. She couldn't afford to think about Lucas Darien on a personal level.

Penny stepped under the heavy jet of the shower and turned her face up towards the razor-sharp spray in an attempt to clear her mind of the confused warmth of last night. It had just been a pleasurable interlude, nothing more, she reassured herself sternly.

She felt a little better once she had showered and dressed. She continued to give herself a severe pep talk as she dried her hair, and by the time she left Lucas's bedroom had almost managed to convince herself that her priorities were back in order. Then she walked downstairs into the kitchen, her eyes connected with Lucas's and all her stern words counted for nothing.

'Good morning.' He smiled at her and she felt as if someone had pushed her into orbit, leaving her stomach behind.

'Morning.' She gave him the briefest of smiles and then wrenched her eyes away from his, trying very hard not to remember how they had wished each other good morning earlier... She was glad that they weren't alone in the room; Isobel was sitting at the breakfast bar, a glass of milk in front of her.

'How are you this morning, Isobel?' she asked, turning her attention to the child.

Isobel barely looked up. 'I'm okay,' she murmured.

'I'm making Isobel's favourite breakfast of pancakes,' Lucas said with a smile. 'Would you like some?'

'No, thank you. I never really eat much breakfast.'

'They won't be as good as Mrs Gordon makes anyway,' Isobel told her.

'Of course they will. Bet I make the best pancakes you've ever tasted,' Lucas said. 'Go on, try some, Milly. You must be hungry.'

Hidden in the softly spoken words was the husky reminder of why she should be hungry.

'No, I'm fine—really.' Penny hoped her cheeks hadn't just flared with colour. 'But I'll make some tea, if you don't mind.' Without waiting for him to reply she headed over for the kettle. She'd just have a quick drink and get back to the office. A cosy breakfast was definitely not what she needed right now.

'That would be great,' Lucas said cheerfully. 'But I'll have coffee.'

'Fine.' She busied herself opening cupboard doors to find cups.

Lucas poured some batter into a pan and the gentle sizzle of cooking filled the air. Surprisingly he looked quite at home in front of the stove, she thought as she glanced over at him. He was dressed in casual faded blue jeans and a blue T-shirt, and he had a teatowel strung over one shoulder, as if he spent most mornings whipping up some gastronomic delight. As Penny watched he scooped up the edges of the pancake and then flipped it over expertly.

'Mrs Gordon would be most impressed,' she remarked, and grinned over at Isobel, expecting her to smile back.

But Isobel was sitting at the breakfast bar looking totally unlike her usual sunny-natured self. She was resting her chin in her hands, a look of total dejection on her young face.

Penny looked questioningly over at Lucas and he shook his head.

'Isobel's grandma has had to cancel their outing today,' he explained in a light tone. 'She's a little disappointed.'

'Oh, dear.' Penny glanced back at Isobel. 'A little disappointed' was obviously the understatement of the year.

'Gran was going to take me to the beach,' Isobel said in a low tone.

And, judging by the pretty yellow pedal-pushers and matching top, she had been all ready to go when the news came. There was even a beach bag on the floor beside her, packed with a towel and her bucket and spade.

'That's a shame,' Penny said sympathetically. 'Maybe she'll take you another day instead.'

'Maybe...but she isn't feeling very well.' Isobel frowned, her young face suddenly creased with concern. 'I hope she doesn't have to go into hospital like Mrs Gordon.'

'I don't think she will, honey,' Lucas said quickly. 'Now, do me a favour—will you go outside and call Flint in?'

'Flint isn't allowed in the kitchen. Mrs Gordon says so,' the child told him solemnly.

'Well, we will make an exception today, as it is special circumstances,' Lucas said easily.

'Okay, Daddy.' The child slipped down off the high stool and ran out of the back door. A few seconds later they could hear her calling for the dog.

'That's better—thought we could do with a minute on our own.' Lucas smiled. He put the teatowel down and switched the cooker off, and in the ensuing silence Penny could feel her heart drumming erratically against her chest as he crossed purposefully towards her.

He looked so handsome and sure of himself, and suddenly she wasn't sure of anything any more...except the fact that all her strong words were like dust in the wind as soon as he came close.

He smiled at her. 'So, how are you feeling this morning?'

'Fine.' Vivid memories from last night flitted disturbingly through her mind as their eyes connected. His hands caressing over her waist and then sliding upwards towards her breast...his mouth hot and deeply possessive against her skin. 'Absolutely fine,' she reiterated brightly, trying to ignore the recollections. How did he manage to look so devastatingly handsome in just blue jeans and an open necked T-shirt? she wondered distractedly. But then Lucas would probably look good dressed in sackcloth, she thought, trying to switch her mind away from the dangerous attraction she felt for him.

'It's a pity Isobel's outing has had to be cancelled,' she said, trying desperately to keep her mind on more sensible things.

'Yes...it is.' He seemed to be studying her very intently; his eyes were moving over her face in a way that sent tingles of pure sensual awareness trickling through her.

Just the way he was looking at her made her want to forget everything and melt into his arms again; the need was like a raw ache inside her. With difficulty she made herself step back from him and forced herself to concentrate on Isobel. 'She seemed very disappointed.'

For a moment she thought he wasn't going to follow her lead, thought he was going to switch the subject back to what had happened between them last night again, but after a brief hesitation he took up the conversation. 'Yes, and unfortunately Pam is cancelling more and more frequently these days.'

'Is her health very bad?'

Lucas shook his head. 'Quite the contrary; she's in wonderful health. Pam's problem is that she has got a new boyfriend who is half her age and apparently she hasn't told him that she is a grandma. She's frightened it might put him off her.'

'I see.' Penny pulled a face. 'He wouldn't be a very nice person if a little thing like that put him off her. Grandmas are getting younger and younger these days anyway.'

'That's exactly what I told her, but she is completely besotted with him and doesn't want to take any risks with the relationship. So I'm afraid Isobel will have to take a back seat for the time being.' Lucas shrugged. 'That's her prerogative. And I wouldn't mind so much if she didn't keep letting Isobel down. She rings her up and makes promises and then at the last minute cancels them because he's arrived. You can't do that with young children; they don't understand. I've had to lie and tell Isobel she isn't well…and I don't like doing that.'

'It's a difficult situation, but you are right—you shouldn't make promises to children unless you are prepared to keep them.' Penny agreed completely. 'I'm surprised Isobel's grandma isn't more sensitive towards her. You'd think losing her daughter would make her granddaughter extra special.'

'You'd think so, wouldn't you?' Lucas agreed dryly.

'Maybe it's the grief of losing her daughter that has made her like that?' Penny suggested lightly. 'Grief can affect people in very different ways, you know.'

'Maybe.' Lucas smiled at her.

'What are you smiling at?' she asked curiously.

'You.' Lucas took a step closer to her, a gleam of humour in his dark eyes. 'You like to see the good in people, don't you?'

'I don't know...do I?' Her heart was starting to thump a heavy and irregular beat again.

'I think so.' To her consternation he suddenly reached out and pulled her into his arms. 'You have some very lovely traits.'

Penny wanted to pull away from him, but she couldn't. The merest touch of his body against hers made her feel weak with longing. She didn't know if she did see the good in people...all she knew was that she wanted to forget that he was her father's enemy and see the good in him.

He stroked the side of her face lightly with his fingers. 'And while we have this moment let me just tell you that last night was wonderful,' he murmured huskily.

Suddenly she didn't know if she could go on with her charade a moment longer. It was burning her away inside. 'Lucas, we need to talk—' She didn't know what she had been going to say, but whatever it was it was curtailed as the back door opened and Isobel came back in, with Flint skipping by her feet.

Lucas stepped back from Penny immediately, and then

bent to stroke Flint as the dog jumped up at him, wagging his tail.

'Look what I've got,' Isobel said, holding out a bunch of daisies in each hand. 'One is for Mrs Gordon and one for Grandma...and...' With difficulty she separated the bunch and held out a few blooms for Penny. 'These are for you.'

'They are lovely, Isobel,' Penny said, touched at the child's consideration. 'Thank you—it's a beautiful thought.' She took the daisies from her and put them to her nose. They had a peppery sweet smell.

'Daddy buys flowers for people sometimes,' Isobel said solemnly. 'He got roses for Emma.'

Penny wondered who Emma was... Some girlfriend, probably; in the language of flowers roses were for love. Was Lucas in love with someone else? She remembered Shauna telling her that he was cut up about a relationship that had just ended. Maybe he still was...maybe last night when he had been making love to her he had been wishing that he was with Emma. She was surprised to feel a sudden fierce surge of jealousy at the thought. The emotion shocked her. She had never been a jealous person and she had no right to feel that emotion now. Lucas could see whoever he wanted...send roses to whomever he wanted...it was none of her business.

'Let's put these flowers in water so they will stay fresh,' Penny said, turning her mind away from Lucas and his dalliances. He probably bought roses for lots of women...probably had a different girlfriend falling at his feet every week.

'There are jam jars under the sink,' Isobel offered helpfully.

Penny went to get them out. The white flowers made

charming posies in the jars. Penny lined them up on the kitchen window ledge and then returned to making Lucas some coffee and herself a cup of tea.

'Do you think Grandma might come and take me to the beach later today?' Isobel asked hopefully as she sat back at the breakfast bar.

'I don't think so, pumpkin.' Lucas put the plate of pancakes down in front of her.

'Oh.' Isobel stared at the plate of food in front of her dejectedly.

'Would you like maple syrup or lemon and sugar to go with those?' Lucas asked.

'Maple syrup, please. Do you think Gran will take me to the beach next week?'

'I don't know. I wouldn't bank on it, Issy.'

Isobel bit down on her bottom lip.

'Have you heard any news about Mrs Gordon?' Penny asked, changing the subject as she put Lucas's coffee down in front of him.

'Thanks, Milly. Yes—I rang this morning. She had a comfortable night and she is waiting for the specialist report this afternoon. Her sister is with her.'

'Can we go and see her, Daddy?' Isobel asked. 'I want to give her my flowers.'

'Not today, Issy. Mrs Gordon needs to have some rest.'

'Will Mrs Gordon still be able to take me shopping for my fairy outfit tomorrow after school?' Isobel asked suddenly.

'I don't think so, Isobel. I think you'll have to make do with my help for that shopping trip.'

Isobel looked shocked. 'Don't be silly, Daddy. You won't know what to buy. That's girls' stuff.'

'I think I might know a bit about what the more fashionable fairies will be wearing this season.' Lucas grinned. 'You can count on me.'

Penny laughed at the absurdity of the statement, but Isobel didn't look amused or impressed. 'You won't know anything! Everyone else will have the right clothes but I won't! Gina Fredrick will make fun of me and everyone will laugh.'

'Oh, come on, Isobel, you are blowing this thing out of proportion. It's a school play and you are six years of age. It doesn't really matter what you wear. All you need is a frilly frock and a wand; nobody is going to laugh at you.'

'Yes, they will—Gina Fredrick will.' Isobel suddenly looked as if she was going to cry. 'Gina won't be wearing a frilly dress. Her mummy takes her shopping all the time and she always looks good.'

'You always look good.'

'No, I don't. I had the wrong shoes for our school walking trip last Tuesday. Gina said they were old-fashioned.' Suddenly Isobel pushed her chair back from the breakfast bar and ran out of the room.

Lucas grimaced. 'Sorry about this, Milly. I think Isobel has had one disappointment too many for one day.'

'It's understandable,' Penny said lightly. 'But I don't think you should have told her that it doesn't matter what she wears for her big event. Even at the age of six a girl knows that's not true.'

Lucas raked a hand distractedly through his hair. 'It's a school play, Milly…'

'Even so, it's important that Isobel feels she is fitting in with her contemporaries. I remember when I went to school how important it was for me to fit in, and I think the pressures on children are even worse now.'

'I suppose you are right.' He shrugged. 'But, hell, if

she is worried like this at the age of six, what the heck will she be like when she becomes a teenager?'

Penny's heart went out to him; it couldn't be easy bringing up his daughter on his own. 'If you want, I'll take her shopping tomorrow.' She hadn't even realised she was going to make the offer until the words were out.

'Would you?' Lucas looked surprised—as well he might. She felt pretty surprised herself. 'That would be very kind of you, Milly. I'd really appreciate it.'

What the heck was she doing? Penny wondered dazedly. This was a real grey area. All right, she sympathised with Lucas's plight—being a one-parent family was not easy, and little Isobel's dejected face had tugged at her heartstrings; at the tender age of six she was obviously conscious of not having a mother, like the other girls in the class—but under the circumstances she couldn't afford to get involved here. This wasn't her problem. And yet...

'You really don't mind?' Lucas checked.

What if Mildred Bancroft turned up tomorrow? Penny's inner voice asked sternly. What then? Not only would she be in deep trouble, but Isobel would be let down yet again by another adult in her life. She should be concentrating on hiding those papers for her father and getting out of here—nothing else.

Penny glanced over at the doorway and saw Isobel's face peeping in; she had obviously heard Penny's offer and was waiting expectantly for her answer.

Penny took a deep breath. 'No, I don't mind,' she said gently. And, strangely enough, she really didn't. What that meant, she didn't know. At this point in time she didn't want to analyse anything too deeply.

She heard Isobel give a whoop of joy and then the

child came hurtling through the door to fling herself at Penny. 'Are you really going to come shopping with me?' she asked excitedly.

'Yes, Isobel. I'll take you tomorrow.' If she'd had any reservations about what she was doing they seemed to evaporate as the little girl climbed up on the stool beside her and flung her arms around her.

'Thank you...thank you,' she squealed excitedly.

'That's okay.' Penny felt quite overwhelmed by the child's response. After all, under different circumstances she wouldn't have thought twice about helping out.

'My dress is going to be far better than Gina Fredrick's now,' Isobel said with triumph.

'Well, I hope so.' Penny laughed. Over Isobel's shoulder her eyes connected with Lucas's. He smiled at her and she felt her heart dip, as if someone had opened a trap door and she had fallen through it.

She hoped he wasn't getting the wrong idea. All right, she liked his daughter, and wanted to help out, but she didn't want him to think that she was harbouring any serious thoughts about the nature of their relationship.

As the child pulled away Penny tried to get into a more businesslike frame of mind. She glanced at her watch. 'I could do with going back to my hotel for a change of clothes before we start work today, Lucas. I'll ring for a taxi—'

'I'll bring you down.' Lucas waved a hand as she started to object. 'I've got to go out anyway. I want to drop those papers at Salvador's house. Get him to check them out.'

Just thinking about those deeds nestling in Lucas's filing cabinet brought a sharp taste of reality into Penny's mouth.

'Tell you what—we'll have lunch at the Smugglers'

Inn and a walk along the beach while we are out,' Lucas continued, and smiled at Isobel. 'That way you can try out your bucket and spade after all.'

Isobel gave another whoop of delight that set Flint barking excitedly.

'Maybe you could give me a key for the house, Lucas,' Penny suggested tentatively over the noise. 'That way I can make my own way back here from the hotel after I've changed, and get on with finding the other documents you need.'

'Time enough for work later this afternoon,' Lucas said easily. 'Have lunch with us, Milly.'

Penny's heart thumped uneasily. Lunch sounded incredibly tempting. But she couldn't afford to relax; her ultimate goal had to be to find those papers. 'You really need those other papers, Lucas, and—'

'The other papers can wait a few more hours,' Lucas said, finishing his coffee.

She supposed he could afford to take a more relaxed view of things now he had the deeds to her father's property safely in his possession, Penny thought wryly. If only she had found them first. She could have been out of here before dinner last night and safely at the airport by now.

'So, what do you say? Will you have lunch with us?'

'Well, I...'

'Please come, Milly,' Isobel entreated, her eyes wide with excitement.

Penny glanced from the child back over at Lucas. 'You are on a time limit to find those papers,' she reminded him shakily, trying not to weaken but to think sensibly.

'I might not need them anyway. It will all depend on what Salvador tells me once he has gone through this other paperwork.'

'I see…' In which case her chance for helping her father might have passed, and it might be time to just cut her losses and book herself on the next flight back to Arbuda to help her father pack up his house.

She glanced from Isobel's earnest face to Lucas, who was patiently waiting for her to answer him. And suddenly the thought of leaving here was unbearable. She'd give herself two more days, she decided. And in that time she could see what the developments were with Lucas's solicitor and she could take Isobel shopping.

'Lunch sounds great,' she said decisively. 'I'd love to join you.'

CHAPTER SEVEN

IT WAS one of those halcyon days that came so often in the Caribbean. Clear blue skies and sizzling temperatures, with just a little edge of a cooling breeze from the trade winds. It was perfect—or rather it would have been if she'd been here under the right circumstances and the situation had been different.

Penny wondered what would have happened if she had told Lucas the truth this morning. Would she be sitting next to him in this car now as he drove her back to her hotel? Or would a taxi have been summoned and the door slammed behind her?

She glanced around at Isobel, who was sitting in the back. Flint was next to her on the car seat and she had her arm around him, happily telling him about their plans for the day. The dog was panting heavily, wagging his tail as if he understood exactly what she was saying.

'They're the best of friends,' Lucas said with a grin as she returned her attention frontward.

'Certainly seem to be,' Penny agreed. 'He's a great dog.'

'Yes, and a good guard dog—he's very protective of Isobel.'

They reached the outskirts of the city and drove down towards the old quarter. Bumping over the cobbled streets, Lucas pulled up a little way from her hotel.

'Do you want to go and see your solicitor and pick me up later?' Penny asked, reaching for the door handle.

'No, we'll wait. It will save me doubling back on myself—and anyway I'd like you to meet Salvador and his wife Maria; they are a nice couple.'

Under the circumstances Penny would have preferred not to meet Lucas's solicitor. 'Well, I might be a while, Lucas.'

'That's okay—we'll wait.'

Short of saying she just didn't want to meet Salvador there was nothing else she could do but nod her acceptance and climb out of the car.

Was it her imagination or was she getting more deeply embroiled in this charade with every passing minute? What with last night... Swiftly she tried to turn her mind away from that...and Isobel...and now Lucas's friends...

She turned into the cool air-conditioned foyer of the hotel and tried not to think too deeply about the situation.

'Morning, Ms Kennedy.' The woman behind the desk greeted her cordially, but it set Penny's nerves completely on edge. Just say Lucas had decided to come into the hotel with her—the game would definitely be up now.

With difficulty she put a smile on her face. 'Call me Milly,' she told her firmly. 'Everyone does.'

'Because of your writing name?'

Obviously the man she had spoken to yesterday had spread the word. 'Yes, that's right. Any messages for me?' she asked, quickly changing the subject. Not that she was expecting any messages. Her father thought she was working on board ship and she hadn't told her work colleagues or friends where she was going.

'No...no messages.'

'Okay, thanks. Could I have my room key, please?'

When she reached her bedroom she stripped off her clothes and hurriedly riffled through her wardrobe and found a cool blue summer dress to wear. Then she decided she'd better ring her father and see how he was.

So she took her mobile out of her bag and keyed in his number. As she waited for him to answer she walked through to the bathroom and brushed her teeth.

He still hadn't answered by the time she had finished. She hung up with a frown, wondering where he was. Maybe he was busy out in the fields. It was a little early, but he might be harvesting the sugar cane around now. She sincerely hoped so, because it would mean he could start paying Lucas some more money next month. And if the price of sugar had gone up and the harvest was good maybe he would get another year in his house. Of course if Lucas got his way and served his papers on time it wouldn't matter what the harvest was like; her father would be finished.

With those sobering thoughts ringing through her mind Penny returned outside to Lucas and Isobel.

'You weren't long at all,' Lucas said as she slipped back into the seat beside him.

'Well, I tried not to be.' She noticed the admiring glance he sent in her direction before he slipped the car into gear and pulled out into traffic. It had only been the briefest of looks but it had been purely sexual, and it sent an answering heat of desire racing through her.

Don't think about that, she told herself fiercely. Last night could never happen again. Her eyes were drawn to his hands on the steering wheel…large, capable hands that had caressed her so passionately, taking her to wild heights of exhilaration.

'We've had a slight change of plan while you've been in the hotel,' Lucas said, changing down a gear so that the powerful car could negotiate the winding roads more easily. 'I rang Salvador and he's just driving his mother-in-law home, so I said we'd have lunch and a walk first, then call on him for coffee on the way back.'

'That's fine,' Penny said, relieved that her meeting with his solicitor was being deferred, even if it was only for a few hours.

After travelling a few miles Lucas parked the car at the edge of a headland. 'The restaurant is over there,' he said, pointing to a white building in the distance that sat at the edge of a creamy white bay lined with palm trees. 'We can walk along the beach to it from here, if you are up to it?'

'Of course I'm up to it,' she said indignantly. 'It's not that far.'

He grinned. 'Just checking that you aren't too tired after your disturbed night's sleep.'

She felt herself blush to the roots of her hair and he laughed.

'I don't know what is so funny about that remark,' she said stiffly.

'Don't you?' His grin seemed to stretch even wider. 'You should see your face.' He reached for the door handle. 'So much for the modern, it-means-nothing remarks last night.'

'I meant what I said last night,' Penny replied, and her voice was quiet and steady but her heart was thumping with rapid disapproval.

'Whatever you say.' Lucas smiled. 'But I get the feeling you are more old-fashioned in your outlook than you like to let on.'

'Milly isn't old-fashioned,' Isobel piped up innocently from behind them, reminding them both of the young ears that might not have understood what they were talking about but were listening in just the same. 'She's cool.'

'Thank you, Isobel.' Penny smiled at the little girl, touched by her intervention. She glanced over at Lucas and couldn't resist grinning back at him and adding the childish words, 'So there.'

'You women always stick together, don't you?' he drawled with teasing amusement.

'That's because little girls are made of sugar and spice and all things nice, and little boys are made of slugs and snails and puppy dogs' tails,' Penny said with wink in Isobel's direction. 'So we have to stick together, don't we, Isobel?'

Isobel giggled. 'Yep, I reckon.' She nodded her head.

Together they got out of the car and walked towards the beach. 'Colin Sal is the naughtiest boy in our school, and he is definitely made of slugs and snails,' Isobel told Penny, taking hold of her hand as they walked down a winding path under the shade of palm trees. 'He brought a huge cockroach into school in a matchbox and let it loose in Miss Jenkins's desk and it ran up her sleeve.'

'Ugh.' Penny cringed. 'Poor Miss Jenkins!'

'I know.' Isobel nodded, pleased with Penny's shocked reaction. 'And it was huge,' she added dramatically. 'About that big…' She held up her hand to indicate a length of about six inches. 'Miss Jenkins was nearly crying.'

'I bet she was.'

'He's not a very nice boy,' Isobel added solemnly.

'Maybe you'd better keep your distance from him, then?' Penny suggested with a smile.

'Maybe…' Isobel let go of her hand as they reached the end of the path and ran ahead to cut across some rocks. Flint bounded across them with her, wagging his tail and waiting for her as he jumped down on the sand ahead of her.

'Be careful on the rocks,' Penny called after her.

'I will,' she called back merrily, without checking her speed.

'Slow down, Isobel,' Lucas called firmly as he watched her leap from rock to rock. She altered her stride slightly and jumped down onto the sand. 'I tell her to go carefully on there every time we come and she still insists on racing ahead.' Lucas reached out a hand to help Penny as they started to follow her across the rock surface.

'I'll be okay.' Penny slipped off her high-heeled sandals and, ignoring his hand, followed in Isobel's footsteps. Only when she reached the other side did she hesitate. The leap down onto the sand was quite steep.

Lucas jumped down ahead of her and then reached up to help her. Rather than topple down in an ungainly fashion she accepted the help, taking hold of his hand and then gingerly slipping down. He steadied her as her feet connected with the ground and for a moment she was held close against his body. Immediately her senses responded to that closeness. She was aware of the deliciously familiar tang of his cologne and the strength of his arms around her. She glanced up uncertainly and their eyes met. The yearning to be even closer and to feel his lips against hers was intense.

He was the one to step back from her. 'It's a bit of a step down, but worth it for the walk,' he said lightly, as if he hadn't been aware of the instant sexual chemistry that had flared.

Maybe he hadn't, she thought. Maybe last night he had enjoyed his fill of her and was now content to light-heartedly draw a line beneath the episode. She wished she was…but shockingly her traitorous body still seemed to be clamouring for more.

For a while they walked in silence, watching Isobel as she skipped ahead of them, her pink bucket and spade in one hand, the other resting lightly on Flint's head. The sand was warm under Penny's feet, the sun dazzling over the turquoise water. There wasn't another person around for miles.

'It's beautiful here,' Penny said, taking a deep breath of the salt-laced air.

'Just what we needed after being cooped up in that office,' Lucas agreed.

Isobel came running back to show them a shell she had picked up.

'That's very pretty.' Penny took it from her, admiring the pink mother-of-pearl sheen. 'You should keep it—put it on your dressing table and it will always remind you of our perfect day together on the beach.'

'I'll put it on top of my jewellery box,' Isobel said, pleased with the idea. 'Will you keep it safe for me?'

'I will indeed.' Penny opened her purse and put it in.

'You're very good with her,' Lucas remarked casually as they walked on again, Isobel skipping happily ahead. 'You seem a natural around children; I'm surprised you haven't got some of your own.'

'I would like a family one day,' Penny admitted, then, for some reason slightly embarrassed by the admission, added hastily, 'In the distant future, I mean…when I'm ready for settling down.'

'Of course.' He smiled over at her. 'So, tell me—have you ever come close to settling down?'

'Yes, once.'

'But you didn't love him enough to commit?' Lucas hazarded a guess when she didn't continue.

'No. I did love him.' Penny frowned. Usually when she talked about Nick or even thought about him there was a deep feeling of pain and regret inside her, but strangely this morning she felt no sharp jolt…no sadness at all. 'I was crazy about him,' she added. 'We lived together for over a year and were planning to get married.'

'So what happened?'

'Nick wasn't as committed to our relationship as I'd thought. He was seeing someone else.' Penny shrugged. 'So I moved out and she moved in.'

'How long ago was that?'

'Almost two years.'

'So, would you say you are over him now?' Lucas asked curiously.

'Yes, of course.'

Lucas noticed the way her green-gold eyes darkened as she spoke, the way her eyelashes flickered down, hiding the emotions within.

'I heard from a mutual friend not so long ago that they got married last Christmas.'

'And do you wish them well?'

Penny slanted a wry glance over at him and for a moment her eyes glinted with humour. 'I was a bit disappointed that they didn't invite me to the wedding. But apart from that there's no hard feelings.'

Lucas laughed. 'Well, obviously the guy is a total idiot.'

'Obviously,' Penny agreed dryly. 'Or maybe he just realised something I didn't…like we weren't meant for each other.' She looked away from Lucas, out across the sea. 'I used to think he was my perfect other half…that meeting him was kismet…'

'And then when it all fell apart you thought your chance for happiness has gone?' Lucas finished the sentence for her and she looked round at him in surprise.

'That's how I felt when Kay died. But life goes on, and surprisingly you can find happiness again. Although

I have to admit to the odd moment of feeling guilty about that…especially in the early days when I started to take a woman to my bed again.'

'I'm sorry, Lucas.' Penny shook her head. 'I'm talking about a mere affair and you've lost your wife.'

'You lived together; that's a lot more involved than a mere affair.'

'Yes…' Penny's heart slammed uncomfortably against her chest. Not a lot of people had understood that…but Lucas did. He seemed so honourable…so decent—and she was deceiving him. She swallowed hard on a lump in her throat.

They were reaching the other end of the beach now, and Penny could see the restaurant quite clearly. Tables with pristine white tablecloths were laid out on a long terrace under the shade of a vine-covered canopy.

'We get the best of both worlds here,' Lucas said as he allowed her to proceed up some steps ahead of him. 'The perfect service and food of a top restaurant along with the informality of beachside dining.'

Penny smiled, but inside she was thinking along much deeper lines—such as the fact there was no such thing as having the best of both worlds. At this moment her father was probably working hard in the fields, worrying that he was going to lose everything and that his efforts were going to be in vain. Meanwhile she was here, having lunch with the enemy. Guilt licked through her. Was she for or against Lucas? She wished she could make a decision and stick with it. All this changing her mind and her sympathies back and forward between the two men was tearing her apart.

All right, Lucas's father had been a rogue and a con-man; there was no doubt about that. But that didn't mean Lucas was from the same mould. On the other hand, there was no doubt that her father didn't deserve to be in the mess he was in.

Lucas pulled out a chair for her, and then sat down opposite.

Isobel was still playing on the beach; she was busy making sandcastles by the water's edge, with Flint patiently watching her every move.

'Shall we leave Isobel to enjoy herself a little longer while we survey the menu?' Lucas asked, and she nodded in agreement.

'We won't leave her too long, though…' Lucas grinned. 'As you missed sampling my wonderful pancakes this morning you must be starving.'

'You're right—I am.' She looked across at him and smiled. 'I was impressed with your culinary skills this morning, by the way.'

'Maybe you'll stay and sample them next time,' he drawled teasingly.

Penny was glad that the waiter appeared beside them at that point, because she honestly didn't know how to respond to that remark. Okay, she knew Lucas was joking around, but she still found the subject of last night difficult to come to terms with. There wouldn't be a next time because it had probably been one of the most foolish moves of her life…it had also been the most pleasurable.

As the waiter greeted Lucas warmly and they talked for a little while her eyes moved over the lean, handsome lines of his face. Lucas was one of the most fascinating and most attractive men she had ever met. She liked the way his eyes lit up with warmth and humour as he talked, and the way there was a slight dimple in his chin when he smiled. Her eyes moved to the darkness of his hair and she remembered the way she had laced her fingers through it as his lips plundered against hers in a sensual moment of complete intimacy, their naked bodies en-twined.

He looked over at her and smiled and her heart vio-lently skipped a beat. 'What would you like to drink, Milly?'

'Er…a glass of white wine, please.' Hastily she lifted up the menu and pretended to study it.

Pull yourself together, she told herself furiously. Last night was just sex…don't dwell on it.

There was silence as the waiter disappeared to get their drinks. The only sound the gentle thud of the surf hitting the sand and the hissing as it withdrew.

'Have you made up your mind what you would like?' Lucas asked after a while.

What she would like was the impossible…she wanted more days like this, more nights like last night… She put the menu down, feeling annoyed with herself. 'I think I'll have the seafood.'

'It's good here—very fresh—'

Isobel came hurrying over to the table and interrupted them. 'Can I have pizza and chips, Daddy?'

Lucas considered the question for a moment. 'That's a bit of an unhealthy combination. Will you eat a side salad with it, and some fruit afterwards?'

Isobel wrinkled her nose. 'I suppose.'

Lucas shook his head as the child ran off again to continue making her sandcastles. 'She'd eat rubbish all day if I let her.'

Penny smiled. 'Wouldn't all children?'

'Probably, but I don't think Isobel would get away with half the things she does if Kay was here. She was always very health-conscious—worked out in the gym, did yoga, ate sensibly.'

'It's a big responsibility bringing her up on your own, isn't it?' Penny said softly.

'Being a single parent isn't easy. And of course with work I have to rely quite heavily on Mrs Gordon. But I enjoy being a dad.' He grinned suddenly as he looked over and saw Isobel paddling into the sea, getting the bottom of her pedal-pushers soaked in the process. 'Well, most days I do anyway.'

The waiter brought their drinks and they placed their order for food.

'You will find it difficult if Mrs Gordon is off work for too long,' Penny reflected. 'What will you do?'

Lucas shrugged. 'I suppose I'll need to hire someone to fill the gap. Not an easy task. Isobel adores her, and she is very reliable. But hopefully it won't be for long.'

Penny sipped her wine and wished she could offer to be of some help. She fought down the feeling, telling herself that she would be helping tomorrow, when she took Isobel shopping. That would have to be enough.

They spent an idyllic couple of hours over lunch. The food was wonderful and Lucas and Isobel were great company. Penny felt very at home with them. It was strange…it was as if she had known them all her life. When Lucas glanced at his watch and told them they should be heading off for Salvador's house it was as if a black thunderous cloud had rolled in over the heat of the day.

'Do we have to go, Daddy?' Even Isobel looked crestfallen.

'Afraid so. And I've got work to do this afternoon, young lady, so you'll have to be good and play quietly.'

Isobel wrinkled her nose.

'Never mind—we are going shopping tomorrow,' Penny reminded her. 'That should be fun.'

Lucas got up to settle the bill and then they headed back across the beach.

'What did you do with the papers for Salvador?' Penny asked, her mind running ahead to the all-important meeting with his solicitor.

'I've locked them in the glove compartment of the car.'

Penny found herself hoping that the car might be gone when they got back. Then pulled herself up fiercely. It was hardly the wish of a decent upright citizen. All right, she wanted things to work out for her father—but not at any price.

And what about the price she was paying? Penny thought suddenly. She glanced across at Lucas. She didn't want to lose his friendship, but ultimately that was what was going to happen.

They arrived at the rocks and he reached out a hand to help her climb up towards the car. 'I really enjoyed lunch,' Penny said, trying to ignore the sensation of pleasure as his fingers curved firmly over hers. 'Thank you.'

'Maybe we can do it again some time. Next weekend we could take the yacht and sail around to a different bay.'

'Maybe.' Penny felt her heart thump painfully. Next week she would probably be back in Arbuda, helping her father. She pulled away from him and followed Isobel up towards the road.

They reached the car and Penny helped Isobel dust the sand off her feet and put her shoes on.

'Thanks, Milly.' Lucas picked up the child's bucket and spade. 'I'm just going to get Flint a drink of water from the back of the car. Will you check in the glove compartment and make sure those papers are all there?' He handed her a bunch of keys. 'It's the small gold one.'

Penny looked at the keys and felt her heart go into

overdrive. Finally she was going to get her hands on the deeds. Was it too late to do anything about it? Or was this the chance she had been waiting for?

Isobel ran around to the back of the car with her father, and Penny sat sideways in the passenger seat to open the compartment.

The papers were in a large brown envelope. She opened it and looked inside. There were reams of pages appertaining to her father's business partnership with Lawrence Darien. And then, behind them, the old yellowed deeds for the Kennedy estate. Just holding them in her hand sent Penny's mind reeling. Could she slip them into her handbag while Lucas and Isobel were occupied with the dog? She could simply tell Lucas they were missing, that he must have left them behind in the filing cabinet... He'd never suspect that she had them...would he?

'Everything in order?' Lucas's voice from the driver's door behind her made her jump nervously. She hadn't heard him coming around the side of the car.

'Yes...seems to be.'

'Great.' He flashed her a smile and then his eyes moved to the deeds in her hands. 'It was a bit remiss of me, leaving them in the car, I suppose.'

'Yes, very careless... But what is it they say? Easy come, easy go?' Penny couldn't keep the dry edge out of her tone.

Lucas's eyebrows lifted slightly. 'I wouldn't say those deeds were that easily come by,' he replied matter-of-factly. 'According to my father he had years of problems with William Kennedy, and gave the guy umpteen chances to pay back what he owes.'

'Really?' Penny had to bite back a terse reply, but there was a wealth of feeling loaded into that one word.

'Yes, really.' Lucas was distracted as Isobel started to giggle and mess about with Flint. 'Come on, Issy, back in the car now.'

Penny had no alternative but to put the deeds away in the envelope. She couldn't take them now that Lucas had seen them in her hand.

'Look, Milly, I know you don't like the thought of evicting someone from their home, and neither do I,' Lucas continued once the child had obeyed him. 'But this is business—not charity.'

'You are really quite cold, aren't you, Lucas?' she said brutally. 'In fact you remind me a bit of a shark circling in the water, the scent of blood around him.'

'It's all very well taking the moral high ground,' Lucas grated sardonically. 'But with respect you don't know the first thing about this case.'

Penny wanted to tell him that in fact she probably knew more than he did about it. But she fell silent.

A few minutes later they were driving back down the road. The light-hearted atmosphere that had accompanied lunch had disappeared.

Penny felt tense, and she could feel the beginning of a headache at the back of her eyes. She glanced surreptitiously over at Lucas. He looked stern and unapproachable now. Obviously her little outburst had not pleased him.

Not that she cared, she told herself. Lucas might be a nice guy, but he was his father's son and blood was thicker than water. And obviously he was going to follow Lawrence Darien's last instructions to the letter, no matter what.

Lucas slanted a look over at her. 'I don't know why we are arguing about this, Milly. I think we should agree to differ on the subject.'

'Fine.' Her tone was airily light.

She was aware that he looked at her rather strangely, and she had to force herself to smile and say lightly, 'As you said, it's none of my business.'

He turned the car through tall, impressive gateposts and up a long and winding drive. A little while later a white bungalow with blue shutters came into sight. It was built on the edge of a steep terraced garden that afforded magnificent views over the Caribbean. But it wasn't the sea view that held Penny's attention, it was the very beautiful young woman who was standing on the door-step. She had long glossy hair the colour of copper beech and was wearing a flowing white summer dress that had crossover straps at the back and a split up the front, show-ing a provocative glimpse of tanned shapely legs.

She turned as their car pulled up beside her, and Penny wondered if it was her imagination or if the woman looked rattled at the sight of Lucas.

'Hi.' Her voice was slightly breathless. 'This is a sur-prise, Lucas. I didn't expect to see you here.'

'Hello, Emma,' Lucas replied as he got out of the car, and it suddenly became clear to Penny why the woman was looking a little uncomfortable. This was Lucas's ex-girlfriend. 'I didn't expect to see you either, but it's a pleasant surprise.' He reached her side and kissed her on the cheek. The woman's skin immediately flushed a bright rosy hue. However, it was the way she looked up at him that really caught Penny's attention.

She's still in love with him, Penny realised immedi-ately. There was no mistaking that look of complete and utter adoration, even though the woman made a brave attempt to try and mask it by stepping back from him and looking hastily away. Where had Shauna got the idea that Emma had been the one to end the relationship?

Penny wondered. From where she was sitting it certainly didn't look that way. But then it was hard to read Lucas; it could be that behind that laid-back, relaxed demeanour he was also cut up about their break-up. Maybe he and Emma had just had a lovers' spat…and she was the consolation prize caught in the middle for one evening. The idea was deeply disturbing. Penny felt a thrust of pain inside her unlike anything she had ever experienced.

Furious with herself, she clenched her hands into tight fists in her lap. Lucas's love-life was nothing to do with her. And it didn't matter that their night together had meant nothing. She had known it could never lead to anything anyway, and was perfectly content for it to be exactly what it was…a pleasurable interlude.

Isobel got out of the back seat of the car and ran over to say hello to the woman.

'Hello, honey.' Emma smiled at her and the little girl smiled back, but stood slightly sheltered behind her father, reaching up to hold on to his hand.

'Maria invited me over for coffee at one-thirty,' Emma said as she reached to pat Flint, who had ambled over towards her.

'Did she?' Lucas looked amused for a second. 'She told me one-thirty for coffee as well.'

'Oh!' The woman looked totally uncomfortable now. 'Look, I had no idea she was planning anything like this.'

'Neither did I, but you know Maria—she has good intentions.'

'I suppose she does. But it's a bit embarrassing, isn't it?' Emma glanced over to the car at Penny. 'Look, I'll go. Tell Maria I'll ring her later.'

'Don't rush off.' Lucas frowned. 'I'm not staying long anyway. I've only come to see Salvador on a matter of business—I've got to get back to work this afternoon.'

'Some things don't change, do they?' She smiled at him wryly.

'No.' He smiled back at her. 'Well, you know me—'

'Focused and dedicated.' She cut across him and then grinned. 'Yes, I know you.'

There was silence between them for a few seconds and they just continued to look at each other.

Penny was starting to feel a bit awkward. She didn't know if she should stay in the car, so as not to intrude, or if she should get out and join them.

'Have you rung the doorbell?' Lucas asked Emma suddenly.

'Oh!' Flustered, the woman reached and pushed the button next to her. 'No! I forgot! I was just about to when you arrived.'

Lucas glanced back towards Penny, as if only just realising that she was still in the car. 'Bring the papers out of the glove compartment, will you, Milly?'

'Certainly, sir,' Penny murmured under her breath as she opened the glove compartment and took out the deeds for a second time that day.

She didn't know why but she felt a tinge annoyed that when Lucas had finally dragged his attention away from Emma it had just been to send a businesslike request in her direction. Maybe it was his way of letting Emma know that she was just a work colleague and nothing more. Well, that was his prerogative, she supposed. And as she wasn't planning on sticking around here for more than a few days more she had no right to feel annoyed by it.

As she got out of the car the front door swung open and an attractive brunette greeted them warmly. 'Lucas and Emma—how lovely that you should arrive together.'

'Well, I think that is more by your design than ours,'

Emma said, reaching to kiss the woman on the cheek. 'I'll forgive you just this once. But only because you are pregnant, Maria. Don't pull an outrageous stunt like this again.'

'Well, you know what they say—the course of true love never does run smooth. And as you two are my dearest friends I just thought you needed your heads banging together…' Maria trailed off in consternation as she suddenly saw Penny walking around the other side of the car. 'Oh…!'

'This is Milly Bancroft,' Lucas interjected smoothly. 'Milly, this is Maria Sandenio and Emma Johnson.'

Taking pity on Maria, who clearly thought she had made a major social gaffe, and to some extent on Emma, who looked as if she was wearing a hair shirt, Penny smiled brightly at them both. 'Pleased to meet you. I'm Lucas's PA.'

'Oh!' Maria looked marginally reassured, but Penny could tell that she still wasn't completely sure what the status was between her and Lucas. 'Well, it's good to meet you too. Come on in—let's not stand out here in the heat any longer.'

Penny handed Lucas the brown envelope as she passed him to go inside and their eyes met briefly. She wondered if he was thankful that she had introduced herself as his PA. After all, if he wanted a reconciliation with Emma it would help clear the path. But it was hard to tell what was going on behind that dark, steady gaze.

CHAPTER EIGHT

SALVADOR met them in the lounge. He was older than his wife; Maria only looked as if she was in her late twenties whilst Salvador was probably in his early forties. His dark hair was tinged with grey at the temples, and he was on the portly side, yet there was a warmth and vigour about him that was immensely attractive.

'Pleased to meet you,' he said, shaking Penny's hand firmly.

Penny smiled back, liking Lucas's friends and wishing again that she were not here under false pretences.

'So these are the infamous papers, are they?' Salvador said, turning to take the envelope from Lucas.

'Yes, we finally unearthed them yesterday.'

'Right—well, let's go through to my study and take a look at them, shall we?' Before anyone could say anything else Salvador had steered Lucas from the room. 'Won't be long, ladies,' he said as he closed the door behind them.

'Now, where have we heard that before?' Emma said to Maria with a grin. 'Do you remember the time when the four of us went to Vieques for the weekend and those two spent the whole afternoon going through some business papers?'

'Vaguely... Now, shall we have tea or coffee?' Maria smiled over at Penny and indicated that she should make herself comfortable on one of the cream leather armchairs.

'Gosh, you must remember that weekend, Maria,'

119

Emma continued, apparently blithely unaware that her friend was trying to change the subject in deference to Penny. 'We had the most wonderful time. It was such a romantic hotel, and Lucas bought me that picture I loved of the old lighthouse at Isabel Segunda.'

'Oh, yes…I kind of remember that.' Maria flicked a narrow-eyed look over at Emma. But she was totally oblivious to it and was settling herself at one end of the settee.

'We were both a bit put out about them bringing work with them, though…weren't we? But that's men for you. Honestly, I'm sure Lucas could stay cooped up quite happily in an office for days on end. When we were dating I used to refer to his work as the other woman…and I don't suppose he has changed any?' She glanced over at Penny for clarification.

'Well…I couldn't say,' Penny murmured. 'I haven't been working for him that long.'

Emma nodded and seemed pleased with the reply.

Penny wondered if the woman was trying to score points by drawing attention to their wonderful romantic weekend, or if she was just still smarting about their split-up and blamed a lot of it on Lucas's work.

'Now, then, what can I get you to drink?' Maria tried again to distract the conversation. 'Cola for you, Isobel?'

Isobel nodded.

'And what about you ladies…tea or coffee?'

'Whatever you are making is fine with me,' Penny said politely.

'Coffee would be great,' Emma said decisively.

As soon as Maria had headed out of the room Isobel sat on Penny's knee and cuddled close against her. 'Can I have lemonade instead?' she asked in a stage whisper.

'I don't know—maybe Maria doesn't have lemonade. Why don't you go after her and ask?'

Isobel shook her head shyly.

'Shall I go and ask for you?'

Isobel nodded, pleased by the suggestion. Emma, on the other hand, suddenly looked annoyed. What was the matter with her? Penny wondered, as she slipped Isobel from her knee.

'So, Isobel…tell me all the news. What's been happening since I've seen you last?' Emma asked in a cosy tone as Penny left the room.

She found Maria opening and closing cupboards in a kitchen that looked out onto a terrace with a spectacular view. 'Sorry to intrude, but Isobel was wondering if she could change her mind and have lemonade?' Penny asked as the woman turned.

'Yes, of course she can.' Maria turned and took a bottle from the fridge. 'Actually, I'm glad to have a moment alone with you. Sorry about before…you know…' The woman looked over at her and grimaced. 'Trying to fix Lucas back up with Emma was a wild idea. I'd no idea he was seeing someone else—'

'You've no need to apologise to me,' Penny said sincerely. 'Really, I'm not in the running where Lucas is concerned.'

Maria didn't look entirely convinced.

'He's a very attractive man, but…' Penny shrugged, and then for some reason—maybe because the woman seemed so genuinely upset at the situation—she found herself confiding in her. 'To be honest, I don't think I'll be staying around here for much longer,' she said, lowering her voice. 'Although I haven't told Lucas that yet.'

'That's a shame. He seems to think very highly of you. I just overheard him talking to Salvador about how invaluable you've been these last few days. How Isobel in particular has taken a shine to you.'

'Yes…I'm going to really miss Isobel.' Penny felt her heart bounce unevenly against her chest.

Maria glanced over at her.

'But things aren't particularly working out for me here,' Penny continued, trying to sound practical. 'So it's best I move on.'

Maria didn't probe further. 'Salvador will be furious with me for inviting Emma today. He is always telling me off for getting involved in other people's problems. It's just I felt sorry for her. She and Lucas seemed to be happy for a while; in fact I hadn't seen Lucas so relaxed since…well, since before Kay died, I suppose. Then with no apparent reason at all he just finished with her. And I was wondering if he really wanted to finish with her or if it was a case of cold feet—maybe he felt he was getting too close to her and panicked. I sometimes think he still feels a bit uncomfortable about dating other women…he was so in love with Kay, you see.' Maria finished loading the tray. 'Does that sound silly? Maybe he wanted to finish with Emma… I'm just guessing.'

'No, it doesn't sound silly,' Penny murmured, remembering how Lucas had that very afternoon admitted to feeling guilty when he'd started to take women to his bed again. 'He could very easily have ended it for those reasons.'

'Well, as Salvador would say, it is none of my business. But really I just want Lucas to be happy. I think he deserves it after all he's been through.'

Penny moved to take the heavy tray from her. 'Here— let me help. I think you are carrying enough around with you,' she added wryly, indicating the very evident bump of her pregnancy.

Maria laughed and patted her bump proudly. 'You're right.'

'When is the baby due?' Penny asked, glad to be able to move to a lighter subject. She didn't want to think about how much Lucas might be in love with Emma...the subject seemed to send her senses into disarray.

'Two weeks tomorrow.'

'Not long, then. Have you got everything packed and ready?'

'Oh, yes. The case is sitting by the bedroom door. Every time I so much as sigh Salvador is looking at me anxiously, wondering if he should run to pick it up and whoo me out to the car.'

Penny laughed. 'I take it nerves are running high?'

'Just a little. I think he's almost more nervous and excited than me.'

Maria opened the lounge door for her.

'Did you have lemonade, Aunty Maria?' Isobel asked shyly as they walked in.

'Yes, honey.' Maria took the glass off the tray and handed it over to her. 'Now, what have you two been talking about?'

'Isobel has been telling me that Mrs Gordon is in hospital,' Emma said, accepting the china cup and saucer that Maria passed over to her.

'No!' Maria looked over at Penny for confirmation.

'She slipped on the kitchen floor last night and Lucas took her down to Casualty,' Penny said with a nod. 'They are keeping her in for observation.'

'Poor woman.' Maria looked upset.

'I wonder how Lucas will manage without her,' Emma reflected, just as the door opened and the men returned.

'I take it you are talking about Mrs Gordon?' Lucas said as he crossed towards the mantelpiece.

'Yes, Milly was just telling us.' Emma looked over at him with concern. 'How will you manage without her?'

'I might have to employ someone else, but hopefully it won't be for long. Thank you, Maria.' He smiled at her as she handed him a cup of coffee.

'Does that mean someone else will be looking after me, Daddy?' Isobel's small voice cut into the conversation. She had a heavy frown across her brow.

'Maybe,' Lucas answered cautiously. 'But only until Mrs Gordon gets better.'

'Will it be somebody I know?'

Lucas shook his head. 'But you soon will know her.'

'But I don't want anybody else.' Isobel suddenly looked as if she was going to cry. 'Unless it is someone I know.' She glanced over at Penny. 'Will you look after me, Milly?' she asked, her eyes wide and pleading, her tone tearful.

Penny was very conscious of everyone's eyes on her, and at the same time her heart went out to the child. She would have given anything to have been able to say yes. 'Well, it's not quite as simple as that, Isobel,' she said instead, softly. 'But your daddy is very clever, and he will find someone really nice for you, I'm sure.'

'Of course I will.' Lucas put his coffee down and went to pick up the little girl and sit down with her on his knee. 'And Mrs Gordon will be back soon.'

Isobel nodded, but her bottom lip was trembling.

Penny wished she could have offered to do more. She glanced over and caught Emma's eyes on her. The woman was staring at her with a look of open resentment.

and it suddenly occurred to Penny that she wasn't at all pleased about Isobel requesting her help.

'So how is work going, Lucas?' Maria asked brightly, trying to change the subject once again. 'You weren't as long in that office as we'd thought.'

'That's because things are fairly much in order.' Lucas rocked Isobel on his knee soothingly. 'Salvador's help is invaluable. I can't thank him enough for squeezing me into his busy schedule.'

'No thanks necessary,' Salvador said swiftly. 'And there is no reason at all why everything shouldn't be settled by the end of the month. As I said earlier, Lucas, now you have those deeds I think you will definitely be taking possession of that land on time, and then the building work can begin. Under Arbuda law once building work has started they won't be able to revoke the permission for it. So if you make an agreement with the contractor who wants to buy the place and allow him access to start immediately there should be no problem.'

Penny felt the blood drain away from her face at those words. She had been worrying about Isobel…about stupid things like did Lucas really love Emma…and her father was about to lose his home. Where were her priorities?

'Are you all right, Milly?' Maria asked her suddenly. 'You look a bit pale.'

Aware that Lucas's eyes were on her, Penny forced herself to smile. 'I've got a bit of a headache, actually, but it's nothing. It will pass.'

'Shall I get you a couple of painkillers and a glass of water?' Maria asked kindly.

'No—really, I'm fine. Thank you.'

'I suppose we should make a move,' Lucas said, glancing at his watch. 'Leave you good folks in peace.'

'You don't have to,' Maria said immediately. 'We were hoping you'd all stay. Salvador was going to light the barbecue later.'

'Another time, Maria,' Lucas said, getting to his feet. 'But thank you for the invitation.'

Everyone stood up and walked with them through to the front door.

Penny noticed that Emma put a hand on Lucas's arm, detaining him. 'If you need any help, Lucas, don't hesitate to call me,' she said in a breathy undertone.

'Thank you, Emma, that's very kind.' Isobel wriggled to get out of his arms and he put her down, allowing her to run outside to where Flint was sitting waiting patiently for them.

'I mean it,' Emma continued earnestly. 'As you know I finish work most days around four-thirty. I'd be happy to look after Isobel for you.'

Penny didn't hear what Lucas's reply was because Flint started to bark excitedly as Isobel ran around the lawn with him. But out of the corner of her eye she did see Lucas bend to kiss Emma lightly on the cheek. She put both hands on his arms and leaned closer and kissed him back.

Hastily Penny averted her gaze completely.

'It was lovely meeting you,' Maria said in a low tone as they stepped outside together. 'And I hope we get to see you again before you leave.'

Penny smiled. 'It was nice meeting you too. And I wish you all the best with your baby. Have you any idea if it is a he or a she?'

'No, it's going to be a surprise.'

'A wonderful surprise,' Salvador agreed, putting an arm around his wife.

As they drove away from the house Penny glanced

back and saw the couple still standing in the garden with their arms around each other, waving. Emma, on the other hand, was nowhere to be seen.

'Your friends are lovely,' Penny said as she settled back and fastened her seatbelt.

'Yes, I think so.' Lucas pulled out onto the road again and they followed the narrow lanes in silence for a while. 'How are you feeling now?' Lucas asked as they approached a junction.

'I've still got a bit of a headache,' Penny admitted, and it was the truth. Her head was pounding with a dull ache—due, no doubt, to tension.

'I'll take you back to your hotel and you can have the rest of the day off,' Lucas said immediately. 'You're probably tired.'

'What about the papers you were anxious to find?' she asked curiously. 'Don't you need them any more?'

Lucas shook his head. 'Salvador says we have enough with what I brought him today to proceed.'

'I see.' Her voice was bleak. So that was that. Her last chance to help her father had definitely passed. And she had squandered a couple of her chances…had been too busy thinking about Lucas when she should have been thinking about her father. Guilt settled like a heavy weight throughout her body. She might as well leave as soon as she could get a flight.

'Will you be well enough to come shopping with me tomorrow?' Isobel asked from the back of the car. And suddenly her guilt was twofold. She couldn't let Isobel down.

'Yes, I'll be fine, Isobel. I'll get a good night's sleep and everything will be better tomorrow.'

Even as she said the words she knew they were far from the truth. Things could only get worse tomorrow.

For a start it was Monday morning and the real Mildred Bancroft might very well turn up. Also, Salvador would probably post the letter of eviction tomorrow and that would end all her father's hopes for the future. Yes, tomorrow could be a very bad day indeed.

Penny fell silent, lost in her own thoughts of the future…a future without Lucas and Isobel.

As Lucas reached the outskirts of old San Juan he was caught up in heavy traffic. The streets were filled with people in colourful clothing and large floats were being brought down the narrow roads. 'There is obviously some kind of festival on today,' Lucas said with a shake of his head. 'We might be a while getting down to your hotel.'

'Just drop me here and I can walk,' Penny said quickly. 'I'd like the fresh air anyway.'

'Are you sure?' Lucas glanced over at her. 'If your head is bad you shouldn't be out in this heat.'

'Really, Lucas, just drop me here,' Penny insisted. 'A walk will do me good.'

Lucas pulled the car away from the crowds and stopped under the shade of an umbrella pine. 'Isobel and I will walk down with you.'

Penny looked into the back seat of the car. 'I think Isobel has had enough excitement for one day,' she said softly.

Lucas followed her gaze and noted that the child was asleep, with her head resting on Flint for a pillow.

'I think you are right.' Lucas smiled.

'Anyway, thank you for a lovely lunch and I'll see you tomorrow bright and early in the office.'

Lucas reached out and caught hold of her arm as she made to turn away. 'Haven't you forgotten something?'

'I don't think so.' Her heart seemed to slam against her chest as she looked back at him, her green eyes wide in her face. Was he going to kiss her? The thought was enough to send her blood pressure soaring.

'Your handbag.' He smiled and picked up her bag from the floor beside her. She couldn't believe that she had nearly forgotten it! It showed the state of her mind.

'Oh, yes! Sorry.' She took it from him, feeling flustered, wondering if he realised she had thought he meant a kiss. 'Thank you.' She reached again for the door handle.

'Milly?'

She looked around at him, wondering what she had forgotten this time. And that was when he leaned closer and kissed her. It was just a light touch of his lips against hers, but the sensation sent wild forces of desire shooting through her, made her senses swim in disarray. In that instant she wanted to move closer and be held in his arms, give herself up to the sheer pleasure of his caresses.

'Thank you for today, and for being so nice to Isobel,' he murmured as he pulled back.

'It wasn't hard,' she whispered in an unsteady tone, trying very hard to pull herself together. 'She's a wonderful child.'

'Well, I think so—but I'm biased.' He grinned.

Something about that lopsided grin made her heart lurch crazily. She stared into the darkness of his eyes. I'm in love with him, she thought suddenly.

The thought shocked her to her core. She couldn't love him—he was her father's enemy. Of all the people in the world to choose from he was the one she couldn't have. Maybe that was why the thought had crossed her mind. She always had been contrary, she reflected angrily.

'Anyway, I'd better go.' She swallowed hard and opened the door. 'I'll see you tomorrow at work.'

'Yes, see you tomorrow.' He watched her climb out

of the car. 'Hope your headache clears. Take some aspirin.'

It would take more than aspirin to clear what was wrong with her, she thought angrily as she walked away from him and merged with the crowds further down the street.

When Penny arrived at her hotel she was glad to find that it was the friendly woman receptionist on duty. She handed over her key without any pertinent remark or question and wished her a pleasant afternoon.

Penny escaped up to her room with a feeling of relief and then lay on the bed looking up at the ceiling, trying to come to terms with the situation.

She wasn't in love with Lucas, she told herself over and over again. And to prove it she lifted the directory next to her and found the number for the airport. Her time here was over. She would book a flight for tomorrow. With determination she lifted the phone next to her bed.

The deed done, she lay back against the pillows. There... Tomorrow at a quarter to midnight she would get on a flight for Arbuda and go home to help and support her father.

The thought should have brought her some comfort. She was finally doing the right thing. She should never have come here in the first place. She imagined what her father would say if he knew...what he would think if he knew she had slept with the enemy! He would be devastated. No...Lucas had never been meant for her. He would be happier with Emma anyway...she was deeply in love with him and seemed genuinely fond of Isobel.

Penny rolled over and buried her head in the pillow and tried to ignore the ache in her heart.

CHAPTER NINE

IT SEEMED unfair that the sun should still be shining when Penny had such a black hole in her heart. Even Shauna's bright, happy good morning grated on her.

'Morning, Shauna.' She gave the girl a strained smile.

'Are you okay? You look a bit pale,' the woman said.

'I'm fine,' Penny lied. In fact she felt anything but fine. Is Lucas in the office yet?'

'Oh, yes. He was in before me, as usual. He's not in a good mood, though, so I would advise you to keep your head down.'

'Really?' Penny frowned; Lucas didn't strike her as a moody person. 'What's wrong with him?'

'Beats me.' Shauna shrugged. 'He was on the phone when I arrived. Maybe it's something to do with that.'

Penny brushed a hand nervously down over her pale pink dress and tried to prepare herself for going into the inner sanctum to face him. She had decided that before he left she should come clean and tell him the truth. That meant saying something either this morning or later today, when she had taken Isobel shopping.

'There is a stack of mail this morning,' Shauna said, going through the pile with a frown. 'We are still very behind with things, thanks to the amount of sorting out since his father passed away.'

'Do you want me to help you go through those?' Penny asked, trying to put off the inevitable. If Lucas was in a bad mood, now was probably not the time to tell him the truth. And anyway, on reflection, maybe it

would be best to tell him after her shopping trip with
Isobel. If she told him before he might cancel the outing
and Isobel would be devastated. Being out here with
Shauna, keeping herself otherwise occupied, seemed an
infinitely better idea.

'Thanks, Mildred.' Shauna passed her half of the correspondence. 'How was your weekend?'

'It was okay,' Penny answered lightly, trying not to
think of the wonderful night of passion and the idyllic
lunch at the Smugglers' Inn. 'What about you?'

Shauna waved her left hand in front of Penny's nose
and she noticed for the first time the big diamond engagement ring on her finger. 'Paul proposed to me.'

'Oh, Shauna that's wonderful—congratulations.'

'Thank you.' The woman had a smile on her face that
seemed to light up the entire room. 'I've never been so
happy in all my life—I adore him.'

'I'm very happy for you,' Penny said with genuine
warmth. 'Have you set a date yet?'

'We are talking about taking the first available one we
can get at the church. I don't want to wait. My mother
is a bit wary, though; she wants us to have a long engagement because we haven't known each other that
long. But I said to her that when you meet the man you
want to spend the rest of your life with you want the rest
of your life to start straight away... And anyway, I just
knew when I first met Paul that he was the right one for
me. I just looked into his eyes and that was it. I was
hooked.'

Penny thought back to when she had walked into the
office last week and had first looked into Lucas's eyes.
Something had happened in that moment, something mo-
mentous. Oh, she had tried to pretend otherwise...had
tried to convince herself that the butterflies and the wild

palpitations were all in her imagination. But they weren't. She was in love with him, had been from that first day. It was crazy and foolish and downright disloyal to her father, but she couldn't help herself. It was the reason she had gone to bed with him on Saturday…and it was the reason she didn't want to tell him who she was because then it would be over. And she didn't want it to be over.

Penny stared down at the envelopes in front of her and tried to be sensible and shut out the thoughts. But they were unfolding in her mind with a relentless certainty that refused to be ignored. Luckily Shauna didn't appear to notice that she had gone extremely quiet. She was telling Penny that she wanted a big white wedding with all the trimmings.

The phone rang, and as Shauna dealt with it Penny sat down on a stool at the far end of the desk and started to go through the mail.

'Lucas Shipping, how may I help?' Shauna said breezily. 'Sorry, he's not in his office at the moment. Can I take your details and get him to phone you back? Okay…no problem.' Shauna put the phone back down. 'Someone else trying to sell us insurance,' she muttered. 'So, anyway, as I was saying, my mother is adamant—' The outer door opened and she broke off as a woman walked in.

'How may I help?' Penny heard Shauna ask politely, but she didn't glance over. She was trying to sort out her priorities at the same time as sort through the mail. Her father had to be her main concern—

'Mildred Bancroft for Mr Darien,' a voice said briskly.

Penny felt her blood start to freeze in her veins and she looked up in horror.

'Sorry?' Shauna was looking at the woman blankly. 'Eh…did you want to see Mildred or Mr Darien?'

The woman frowned. She looked a little like an old-fashioned schoolmarm—the type who peered disapprovingly over heavy-rimmed glasses and gave detention if you so much as sneezed. Her grey hair was tied back in a severe style, away from her lined face, and she wore a plain white blouse and black skirt. 'I think you misunderstand, young woman,' she said in a tone that implied Shauna was slightly thick. 'I am Mildred Bancroft, here to see Mr Darien.'

Shauna's mouth literally dropped open and she looked helplessly around at Penny. If the situation hadn't been so grave the look on her face would have been comical. But Penny wasn't in any mood to laugh. 'You'd better tell Lucas she is here,' Penny murmured numbly.

Before either of them could move the office door opened and Lucas appeared. He looked formidable, his face drawn in a stern expression that Penny had never seen before—an expression that made her stomach knot with even more tension.

'Ah, you must be Mr Darien?' the woman said hopefully. 'I phoned you earlier.'

'Yes…Mildred Bancroft I presume?' Lucas said heavily.

'That's right.' The woman walked around the desk and held her hand out. 'Good to finally meet you.'

'Yes, likewise…' Lucas shook hands with her and then waved her through to his office. For a moment his eyes connected with Penny's. It was a cold, austere look that was a million miles from the way he had looked at her yesterday. 'You can come through as soon as I've dealt with Ms Bancroft,' he told her curtly. It was more of an order than an invitation, and then the door closed firmly behind him.

'Well!' Shauna swivelled around to look at Penny. 'What on earth is going on? And if that is Mildred Bancroft then who are you?'

'Sorry, Shauna.' Penny swept a shaking hand through the long length of her hair. 'It was just that you jumped to all the wrong conclusions when I came in to see Lucas that day, and I was so desperate that I just went along with it.'

'Golly!' Shauna's eyes were so wide they seemed to swamp her face. 'Had you been unemployed for a long time…was that it?'

'No… I just…' Penny shrugged helplessly. She didn't want to start explaining to Shauna before she had a chance to tell Lucas her side of things.

'Look, don't worry about it,' Shauna said softly. 'I'm sure Mr Darien will forgive you, because, let's face it, you're great at the job—things have been so much easier in this office since you arrived.'

'Thanks, Shauna.' Penny smiled at the woman gratefully and wished things were that simple.

'He'd never have employed that sourpuss anyway. At least I hope not!' Shauna made a face. 'Did you see the way she looked down her nose at me? Snooty woman—who did she think she was?'

'She thought she was Mildred Bancroft,' Penny answered dryly, her sense of humour coming briefly to her rescue.

Shauna met her eyes and giggled.

The office door opened at that moment and Mildred Bancroft appeared. Head held high, she marched through the office and without so much as a glance in their direction departed, leaving a freezing trail of mystery in her wake.

The door to Lucas's office was left wide open, but there was no sign of Lucas.

'What do you think happened?' Shauna mouthed silently.

Penny shrugged her shoulders.

'Milly, get yourself in here.' Lucas's voice boomed from within.

A sinking feeling in her stomach, Penny got to her feet.

'Good luck,' Shauna whispered.

'Thanks—I've got a feeling I'm going to need it.'

Lucas was sitting behind his desk, his dark head bent as he scribbled some notes on a form in front of him. 'Close the door,' he said bluntly, without looking up.

She did as he asked and then proceeded cautiously towards the desk. Still Lucas didn't glance up.

'Before you start tearing into me, I just want to say that I'm sorry.' She said the words quickly. 'I shouldn't have deceived you like that. It was wrong of me and I apologise unequivocally.'

Lucas threw his pen down and then leaned back in his chair. Their eyes met.

It was hard to tell what he was thinking. He looked very cool. But it was his silence that totally alarmed Penny. If he had shouted and ranted she probably could have coped better. But this steely look of complete disapproval tore into her like a knife. If he looked at her like this now, what would it be like when he discovered she was William Kennedy's daughter?

'Look, I really am sorry.' She tried again. 'I didn't set out to pretend to be someone else, and I'm not a dishonest person.'

He folded his arms in front of him. 'So who are you?' he asked quietly.

Her heart slammed against her chest and her knees suddenly felt weak. She sat down in the chair opposite to him. 'You can call me Penny,' she said, feebly backing away from telling him her surname.

'Oh, can I?' he grated sardonically. 'How kind. And is this another pseudonym? Is the real Penny about to march in to see me in a few days' time as well?'

'Don't be ridiculous,' she muttered with a flash of annoyance. 'Look, I'm sorry... I did try to tell you that I wasn't Mildred when I came in here last week, but you didn't give me a chance. You were really desperate for someone to help you out in here, don't forget.'

'Oh, and you were just being charitable, were you?' One eyebrow lifted disdainfully. 'Fancied a bit of social work? Hmm, was that it?'

'No...of course not.' She shrugged helplessly. 'I don't know what happened that day. You just looked at me and...I don't know... The next minute I was in this web of lies.'

'I think you've had plenty of chances since then to put me right,' he drawled softly. 'And you didn't take any of them.'

She felt her cheeks flare with colour. 'No...you're right. I didn't,' she admitted shakily. 'But I wanted to.'

'So what stopped you?' He stared at her with a cold, penetrating intensity.

'I suppose the fear that you'd look at me the way you are looking at me now,' she admitted huskily.

There was silence for a moment.

'I just...' She trailed off helplessly.

'Needed the job?' he finished for her wryly.

'Well...I was going to say I just got caught up in the

moment. You asked me if I'd start straight away and I found myself agreeing.' She shrugged. 'It was crazy—I knew the real Mildred would probably turn up sooner or later, but—'

'But you figured you would prove yourself and make yourself indispensable in the meantime?'

'I wasn't going to say that,' she replied, and sent him a fulminating glare from sea-green eyes as her old spirit kicked in. 'Stop finishing my sentences for me.'

'Hey, you are in no position to start dictating terms,' he reminded her crisply, but there was a brief flicker of amusement in his eyes now. 'So I take it the agency sent you and when you got here you discovered the job had already gone. I can understand you being annoyed. You'd travelled a long way to get here. You should have just told me the truth. That agency doesn't seem to know what the hell it's doing. I've been on the phone to them this morning and talked to some woman who was totally clueless. Couldn't even find my file and kept me on hold for twenty minutes. I hung up in the end.'

'They don't seem very professional,' Penny murmured uncomfortably. 'But they are not completely to blame here—'

'Well, they may have a good reputation but I won't be using them again.' Lucas shook his head. 'But you should have been honest. You didn't need to go to so much trouble to get the damn job, as it turns out.' He leaned forwards suddenly. 'Because, given the choice between you and the real Mildred, I would have given you the job anyway.'

'Would you?' She felt her heart speeding up as conflicting emotions spun through her. There was a part of her that didn't want him to start being nice about this—

it just made it even more difficult to tell him the whole truth.

'Where has she been anyway?' she asked distractedly.

'Family commitments kept her in Barbados for longer than she had anticipated.' Lucas shook his head. 'Can you imagine? She actually thought she could waltz in here and start work days late without so much as a phone call of explanation. Anyway, I told her that the agency had sent someone else and that I couldn't afford to sit around waiting for her.'

'Oh!' Penny stared at him in consternation. 'You mean you sent her packing!'

'Well, I wouldn't use those words exactly.' Lucas shrugged. 'We had an amicable meeting. She understood my dilemma. She tried to say that she had written to me, telling me the date she would arrive. But I didn't receive the letter—and anyway, frankly, it's just too late now.'

He tapped his fingers on the desk impatiently. 'Then she had the nerve to tell me that my receptionist wasn't as efficient as she should be.' He frowned. 'A bit of a nerve, don't you think, when she was late for her job? She wouldn't have fitted in here anyway.'

Penny bit down on her lip. 'So...she's not coming back, then?' she ventured cautiously.

'No.' He smiled. 'She's not coming back. I just told you that.'

'I see.' Penny stared at him guiltily. Now she had lost the woman her job! 'Do you think that maybe you've been a bit hasty? Have you got a contact number for her?'

'I don't need a number for her because I won't be contacting her,' Lucas said flatly, and then sat back in his seat. 'So...I suppose what I'm saying is, if you want the job here it's yours.'

Penny sat in stunned silence for a moment. She hadn't expected this. As soon as Mildred Bancroft had arrived she'd envisaged him telling her to pack up her stuff and leave.

'I don't like dishonesty in any form…Penny,' he continued briskly. 'But I've thought about it and I can see you must have been very upset, travelling all that way for a job that had been allocated to someone else. So…' He stood up from behind the desk and walked around towards her. 'I'll overlook your propensity for shady behaviour just this once.' The words were said with a shade of wry humour. He perched on the edge of the desk beside her. 'What do you say? Shall we start from the beginning again?'

Penny would have given anything to just say yes… But how could she? She didn't belong here. She belonged in Arbuda, with her father, or on board the cruise liner doing her own job… This was all a lie. 'It's a bit more complicated than that,' she said huskily.

'No, it's not. You just should have told me the truth up front…Penny…'

The sound of her name on his lips made her heart leap. It sounded so warm and delicious and… She pulled her thoughts back from that dangerous abyss.

'I know I should.' There was a long silence where she tried to pull herself together. She needed to tell him everything. Maybe if she threw herself at his mercy he'd be lenient with her father. And maybe he wouldn't… Maybe it would make things worse for her father. The thought froze her. Lying about her name was bad…lying about what she was doing here was a lot worse. Maybe she should tell him as little as possible and just exit gracefully from the situation. At least that way he wouldn't hate her. She couldn't stand for him to hate her.

'The thing is I'm feeling tremendously guilty that I've lost Mildred Bancroft her job.'

'I wouldn't waste your energy with that,' Lucas said firmly. 'If you hadn't come along when you did I'd have got someone else. I was at the end of my tether waiting for her anyway.' His eyes flicked over her assessingly. 'So, now we have all that cleared up, will you stay on here as my PA?'

Her heart was beating furiously against her ribcage. She moistened her lips nervously and then took a deep breath. 'I can't, Lucas,' she said softly. 'I'm sorry.'

He frowned, and there was a long pause before he said heavily, 'Do you mind telling me why not?'

'I have personal reasons. But I don't think it's working out here for me anyway.' She forced herself to say the words, but her voice was husky and anything but sure.

'Has this got anything to do with what happened between us on Saturday night?'

The direct question and the way his eyes were searching over her face made her blush uncontrollably. 'No...of course not.'

'Are you sure?' he asked gently.

'Of course I'm sure.' His closeness was a little unnerving. If she moved a fraction of an inch her leg would be touching his. And she could smell the evocative tang of his cologne. It brought back memories of being in his arms, running her fingers through his hair, their naked bodies pressed close.

'I suppose businesswise what happened between us was a mistake. But—' He broke off as the phone rang on his desk. 'Shauna, will you hold my calls?' he called impatiently through to the outer office. But the phone continued to ring. 'Shauna—the phone.' He raised his voice an octave and the ringing stopped.

'This is nothing to do with what happened on Saturday night,' she cut in quickly, before he could say anything more. 'I told you…that was just a bit of fun. I've forgotten it already.'

He raised one eyebrow. 'Is that a fact?' he drawled coolly.

'Yes.' Her eyes connected with his for a second before she rapidly looked away.

'I think you are wrong about that,' he said softly. 'It wasn't just a bit of fun.'

The calm, husky timbre of his tone set her pulses racing. She looked back up at him uncertainly.

'It was a lot of fun,' he finished distinctly.

The flare of disappointment inside her was acute, and she realised that deep down she had been hoping he was going to say something else. Stupid of her, really, but in that heartbeat of a moment a whole load of romantic notions had raced through her head—notions of him telling her that their lovemaking had affected him as profoundly as it had her.

Idiot, she berated herself angrily. Their night together had just been a passing distraction, and a man as attractive and as sexy as Lucas probably had a lot of them. If Lucas was going to get serious about anyone it would be Emma.

'Penny?' As she looked away from him he put a hand under her chin and gently tipped her face so that she was forced to meet his gaze again. His eyes held hers, steady and somehow intense. They seemed to reach straight into her soul.

'Will you at least stay on until I can find someone to replace you?' The businesslike question was very much at odds with the gentle tone of his voice, the touch of his hand against her skin.

'I don't think I can,' she whispered helplessly, and pulled away from his touch. But even though she had broken the contact with him her skin seemed to burn from his touch.

There was a tap on the office door. 'Mr Darien, it's the call you have been waiting for from Arbuda,' Shauna said apologetically as she stuck her head around the door. Her glance moved from Penny to Lucas, noting the fact that he wasn't behind the desk but sitting quite close to her.

'Tell him I'll phone him back,' Lucas said calmly.

'I think it's important. He sounded agitated and demanded to speak to you.'

'Tell him I'll phone him back.' This time Lucas's tone brooked no argument and Shauna hurriedly closed the door.

'So, do you want to tell me why not?' he asked Penny, as if there had been no interruption.

Penny took a deep breath and stuck as closely to the truth as she dared. 'My father is in trouble and I need to go home and help him.'

Lucas said nothing for a moment, and the way he was looking at her was unnerving.

'I told you about him, if you remember...'

'Yes, I remember.' He stood up from the desk and returned to his seat. 'Okay I'll give you a couple of weeks off to sort the problem out with your father. But then I need you back here.' Lucas was flicking through some pages in his diary and he spoke like a man who was used to getting his own way. 'I've got an extremely busy period towards the middle of next month. Can you be back by then?' He glanced over at her sharply.

Penny hesitated, then inclined her head. There was no

point in discussing this. She was booked on a flight to Arbuda tonight and she wouldn't be coming back.

'What time do you want me to take Isobel shopping?' she asked instead.

Lucas glanced up. 'I thought we'd finish early and collect her straight from school.'

'Are you coming?' she asked in surprise.

'Of course I'm coming. You need someone to drive and carry shopping bags, don't you?' He grinned.

The phone rang again, and then went dead as Shauna answered it. 'It's the builder again,' she called, a note of desperation in her voice.

Lucas snatched up the receiver. 'Hi, John, how's it going?' he asked jovially. 'Yeah, sorry about that—I was in a business meeting with a wayward member of staff.' He glanced over at Penny with amusement lurking in his dark eyes.

Penny didn't smile back. She was feeling desperately guilty for lying to Lucas, but he didn't feel in the slightest bit guilty about what he was doing to her father. He said he didn't like dishonesty of any kind, but what he was doing was downright wicked.

She scraped her chair back from the desk. The sooner she got away from him and forgot all about him the better.

CHAPTER TEN

ISOBEL spun around and around, her arms outstretched, the white dress billowing out around her legs, her dark hair swinging.

'What do you think, Milly?' she asked excitedly.

'I think you are going to get dizzy and fall over. Stand still for a minute.' Penny grinned.

The child did as she asked and the dress fell in soft folds around her. She looked like a little cherub. The ragged handkerchief hem was perfect and the short sleeves trimmed with strands of seed pearls looked just right. She lifted her face expectantly towards Penny, and her cheeks were rosy and her eyes shone as she gave a cheeky grin. 'What do you think?' she asked again.

'I think you look like the most perfect fairy princess in the whole world.' Penny smiled and then impulsively bent and kissed the child on her forehead.

Isobel threw her arms around her neck and hugged her. 'Wait until Gina Fredrick sees this!'

'She'll be impressed,' Penny agreed. 'And I think your daddy will be impressed too.'

'I am impressed,' Lucas said from behind them, taking them both by surprise. He had poked his head around the door leading to the changing rooms and was looking down the corridor at them.

'You're not allowed in here, Daddy. It's girls only,' Isobel said, wagging a finger at him in disapproval.

'It's only the corridor, Isobel,' Lucas said with a grin.

'I don't think I'll see anything I shouldn't. Come on out so I can look at the dress properly. I'm getting lonely out here.'

Dutifully Isobel trotted outside, into the main body of the shop, whereupon she caused quite a sensation with the assistants who came over to admire her in the dress.

'She looks gorgeous, doesn't she?' Penny remarked quietly to Lucas as she stood next to him and watched the little girl twirling happily in front of the mirrors.

'Yes, she does,' Lucas agreed softly, and then grinned at Penny. 'And you were right—that dress is definitely worth traipsing into every shop in town for.'

'You are learning fast.' Penny laughed. Lucas had been starting to flag as they had rejected one dress after another. In typical male fashion he had been ready to call it a day as they had tried shop after shop. But Penny had been determined that Isobel would get her dress today. She wanted to get on that plane tonight knowing that at least she had achieved something on her trip here…even if it was something as small as making a child happy.

'You've got to have stamina when you go shopping with the girls,' Penny said lightly. 'Isn't that right, Isobel?'

Isobel nodded happily.

'Okay, you've made your point, but it's time to eat now,' Lucas said firmly. 'There is a great little restaurant just down from here—'

'But I haven't got my wings yet, Daddy,' Isobel said. 'I can't be a fairy princess without wings.'

'I don't think we will be able to buy them in a shop, Issy,' Penny said. 'Tell you what—we'll find a haberdashery and buy some wire and some gossamer material and I'll construct you a wonderful pair of wings.'

'There's no end to your talents, is there?' Lucas remarked lightly.

'Not really, no,' Penny agreed with a teasing smile.

He smiled back, and as their eyes locked Penny felt her heart go into freefall. Hurriedly she looked away. She couldn't allow herself to think how handsome he was…how much she wanted him. Because he was out of bounds. She could never have a relationship with Lucas Darien. A gnawing ache caught at her heart, but she firmly tried to ignore it, reminding herself instead that he had spent several hours at the office today looking into the business of evicting her father from his home.

'When will you make my wings?' Isobel asked anxiously.

'I'll do it tonight,' Penny promised.

'You don't have to do it so soon. The play isn't for another three weeks,' Lucas told her.

'Even so, it would be better to get it done now.' Penny smiled at Isobel. 'Then you can relax, knowing you are organised—isn't that right?'

The child nodded happily.

'Okay, well, as you are kindly going to create a costume for my daughter, how about I create some dinner for us back at home while you are busy?' Lucas suggested.

Penny hesitated. Her plan had been to run the wings up in her hotel bedroom and then leave them by Lucas's front door on her way out to the airport. But it seemed much more sensible to make them at his house and then just leave.

Penny nodded. 'You've got yourself a deal.'

Half an hour later they arrived back at Lucas's house, laden down with bags.

'I don't know about you, but I could use a drink,' Lucas said as he put the shopping down in the kitchen.

'You can't take the pace, Daddy.' Isobel giggled.

'You're right—I can't.' He smiled over at Penny. 'How about a glass of wine?'

'Thanks—I'd love one.' Penny took the bag with Isobel's dress in it and handed it over to the little girl. 'Better go and hang that up before it gets creased.'

'Yes, Milly,' the child said happily.

'Isobel?' Penny stopped her as she ran towards the door. 'You can call me Penny, if you like…because all my friends do.'

The child seemed to think about that for a moment. 'I like the name Milly better,' she said. 'Can I still call you Milly?'

'Yes, if you like,' Penny said, puzzled by the request.

'Good.' The child smiled and ran out.

'I wonder what is behind that,' Lucas murmured.

'Beats me.' Penny shrugged. 'Maybe she just thinks it's a bit strange, calling me by a different name.'

'I thought it was a bit strange myself,' Lucas said, a glint of humour in his dark eyes.

'Yes, well, I am sorry about that, Lucas,' she said briskly.

'That's okay.' He uncorked a bottle of white wine and for a moment the only sound was the plump glug of liquid as he filled two glasses. 'I just hope you don't mind if I slip occasionally and call you Milly myself.' He passed the glass over to her and her hand brushed against his as she accepted it. The contact sent an immediate rush of adrenalin racing through her. 'You see, I tend to think of you as Milly. Thoroughly modern Milly.'

She tried to pretend that she didn't know what he was

referring to, but the teasing, sexy tone of his voice sent her senses racing.

'If you slip and call me Milly I won't hold it against you,' she assured him with a half-smile, trying to feign indifference. But when she met his eyes she felt her heart dip as if she had suddenly lost all sense of gravity. If only he knew, she thought poignantly, that there was nothing casual or modern about her feelings for him. That she had slept with him for the most age-old of reasons. She was in love with him.

He smiled and touched his glass against hers. 'And thanks for helping out with Isobel today. I don't know what we would have done without you.'

'I'm sure you would have managed.' She turned and tried to busy herself looking through the bags on the table. 'Now, I suppose I should get on with Isobel's costume.'

'You can work in here on the table, if you'd like,' he said, helping to clear a space for her by taking some of the bags away.

'I don't want to get in the way of your cooking,' she said quickly, thinking it might be easier to concentrate on what she was doing if she was in another room from him.

'Don't worry—you won't be in the way,' he said with a grin. 'And anyway, I could do with some moral support. I'm afraid my cooking is a little rusty. I actually burnt dinner last night, and we were only having hamburgers and salad.'

Penny smiled mischievously. 'Was it the lettuce or the hamburgers that you burnt?'

'Hey, I'm not that clueless.' Lucas took off the jacket of his business suit and rolled up the sleeves of his white shirt. 'And to prove it I shall create a masterpiece,' he assured her. 'I just want a witness, that's all…' He slanted a wry grin in her direction. 'And maybe a bit of advice as I go along.'

'You might be asking the wrong person,' Penny joked. 'My cooking isn't that marvellous either.'

She busied herself emptying the material and the wire onto the table, trying not to notice how attractive Lucas looked. There was something about his casual informality and the teasing smile that just set her senses racing. Out of the corner of her eye she saw him loosening his tie to take it off. She noticed the strong column of his neck, the powerful forearms…

'How's Mrs Gordon?' she asked, trying firmly to steer her mind away from dangerous ground.

'She's okay. I rang the hospital this morning and they said she'd had a comfortable night. The good news is that they are saying now she might not need surgery on her hip, that physiotherapy might fix her up. But she is going to have to take it easy for a few weeks.'

'You'll miss her.'

'You're not kidding.' Lucas opened the fridge and took some vegetables out. 'I'm going to take Isobel in to see her tomorrow night. Come with us, if you'd like.'

'It might not be a good idea, Lucas,' Penny answered carefully. 'She might not be up to having so many visitors at once.'

'Well, I'll check and tell you tomorrow.'

She'd be back in Arbuda tomorrow, Penny thought bleakly. And she would probably never see Lucas or Isobel again.

'How's the repossession order going with the house on Arbuda?' she asked him, firmly trying to concentrate on the reason why she couldn't stay here. She had tried to monitor the situation as she continued to go through files today, but a lot of her work had taken her to the outer office. 'You seemed to be on the phone a lot.'

'That's because there's a lot to sort out.'

'Has Salvador sent out the letter of eviction yet?'

'You sound very disapproving, Penny.' He paused by the table, and when she didn't answer him or look over at him he reached out and put one finger under her chin, forcing her to look at him.

'I am disapproving,' she said cautiously. 'I've told you that already.'

'And I've told you it's just business, Penny. Repossession isn't pleasant, but it happens.'

She stepped back from him angrily. But she was angrier with herself than with him, because despite the unpleasant subject she felt a flare of sexual need inside her at the touch of his hand, the closeness of his body. The fact that she could still feel like that at the same time as talking about her father's downfall was shocking, and she hated herself for it...but she just couldn't seem to help herself.

'Anyway, as you said before, we'll agree to disagree about it, shall we?' she said shakily, trying to cover up her emotions by starting to unravel the roll of netting on the table.

'I suppose you feel strongly about this because you are worried about your own father and his financial problems,' Lucas said suddenly.

The sentence caused her to look over at him sharply. Did he have any idea how close he was to the truth? she wondered, and her heart hammered wildly against her chest. 'I feel strongly about it because I think what you are doing is wrong.'

'For someone who has been...shall we say...

economical with the truth, you can be quite sanctimonious, can't you?'

She frowned. 'Yes, well, I've said I'm sorry,' she muttered shakily. 'And I didn't set out deliberately to lie or to hurt anybody.'

'Look, Penny, my father left me a job to do and I'm doing it.'

And blood was thicker than water at the end of the day, she thought grimly. If she told him his father was a cheat it would not further the cause of softening his attitude in any way. She was frankly wasting her time.

Luckily at that moment Isobel ran back into the room. 'What are we having for dinner, Daddy?' she asked happily.

'Stir-fried vegetables and steak.'

'Can I have chips?'

'No, you can't.' Lucas said.

Isobel made a face. 'Daddy burnt dinner last night,' she told Penny as she climbed up on the stool next to her. 'It tasted horrible.'

'Yes, thank you, snitch.' Lucas ruffled her hair and she grinned.

There was silence for a while as Lucas carried on with the preparations for the meal and Isobel watched Penny. She had probably gone too far in her condemnation of him, she thought as she snipped the wire to size. She wondered if it was her imagination or was there a bit of an atmosphere between them now?

'Do you like my daddy?' Isobel asked Penny suddenly

The question took Penny very much by surprise 'Well…yes…'

'He likes you too,' she said happily. 'Don't you Daddy?'

Penny glanced over at Lucas and met his eyes

Whereas she felt deeply embarrassed by the line of questioning, he merely looked amused. 'Yes—well, most of the time anyway. I could have done without the surprise this morning.'

'What surprise?' Isobel asked.

'Never you mind.' Lucas turned off the stove. 'I'm going to serve dinner now. How long will you be, Penny?'

'I'm just about finished.' Penny glued the last piece of net in place.

'We'll adjourn to the dining room, then. Come and help me lay the table, Issy.'

Lucas was just in the process of carrying the food through to the other room when the phone rang. 'Will you pick that up for me, Penny?' he called back over his shoulder. 'Tell whoever it is I'll call them back after dinner.'

It was Emma, and she sounded distinctly put out when she heard Penny's voice answering the phone. 'You're working late,' she remarked stiffly.

'I was just helping Isobel with a costume for her school play,' Penny told her.

'I see.'

'Lucas is just in the process of preparing dinner—can he ring you back, Emma?'

'I just wanted to tell him that Maria has gone into labour. Salvador took her into hospital this afternoon.'

'That's great news. Although she is a bit early, isn't she? I hope everything goes okay for them.'

'Yes, so do I. Oh, and will you tell Lucas that I said thank you for the beautiful bouquet of flowers? Tell him they were fabulous. I'll call him tomorrow—I'm just on my way to the cinema now.'

'Okay, I'll tell him.' Penny put the phone down

thoughtfully. If Lucas was sending Emma flowers did that mean he wanted to get back with her? She tried to tell herself that it would probably be a good thing if he did. It would mean he had finally put the past and Kay behind him, and Isobel clearly needed a mother figure in her life.

'Penny, your dinner is getting cold,' Lucas called through from the other room.

'Sorry about that,' she said as she went through and took her seat at the candlelit table opposite to Lucas. 'That was Emma; she said that Maria has gone into labour. Salvador is with her at the hospital.'

Lucas grinned. 'Well, that's exciting news. I hope she has an easy time and it all goes well.'

'Yes, so do I.' Penny looked down at the food in front of her. 'This looks very nice.'

'Chips would have been better,' Isobel piped in. 'They are my favourite. Chips and tomato sauce.'

'My daughter has a wonderful taste in fine cuisine, don't you think, Penny?' Lucas said with a shake of his head.

'She certainly does.' Penny winked at Isobel, and then returned her attention to Lucas. 'Oh, and Emma said to say thank you for the flowers. She said they were fabulous. She'll ring you tomorrow; she's going to the cinema tonight.'

Lucas nodded. 'I'm glad she liked them,' he said casually.

Penny pushed the food around on her plate. She had been feeling hungry earlier, but now her appetite seemed to have completely deserted her. The thought of Lucas with Emma was like a knife twisting inside her. The fact that she knew she was being ridiculous just made it all the worse. She was leaving Puerto Rico. There was no way a relationship between her and Lucas would ever work out. Even if he did forgive her for lying to him— and that was a big if—it would certainly break her father's heart if he found out she was involved with Lawrence Darien's son. The whole situation was a complete no-go.

'How's my cooking?' Lucas asked, reaching over to top up her wine glass.

'Surprisingly good.' She smiled over at him. It was a lovely meal; it was just a pity she couldn't enjoy it. 'Mrs Gordon would be proud of you.'

'It's raining, Daddy,' Isobel said suddenly. They all looked towards the window. A torrential tropical downpour was almost obscuring the greenery of the garden.

'Wow! I hope that doesn't stay around for long, otherwise I'll get soaked just running into the hotel.'

'You can always stay here tonight,' Lucas suggested.

The invitation was issued in a casual way but it sent Penny's senses into wild disarray. 'No, I'll be fine, Lucas,' she said hastily. But she couldn't bring herself to look across at him as she replied. Was he inviting her to share his bed again? Or was he simply offering her the spare room? She wasn't sure. But whichever it was she had to remain strong and refuse.

'In fact, I'll help you clear these dishes away and then I really must ring for a taxi. I've got a few phone calls I want to make from my hotel.' She forced herself to say the words, and to sound cool and practical, even though the thought of sleeping with him again was making her blood thunder through her veins with excitement and longing.

'Fair enough.' Lucas nodded his head.

'Daddy, can I be excused now?' Isobel asked.

Lucas glanced down the table, checking how much of

her dinner she had eaten. 'Okay. But it's getting late now, Issy, so you have to start getting ready for bed.'

'Will you come and tuck me in?' Isobel asked.

'Don't I always?' Lucas said with a smile.

'No, I meant Milly…will you tuck me in tonight, Milly?'

'If you like,' Penny agreed softly, touched by the child's request.

'Meantime, it's into the shower with you,' Lucas said as he got to his feet and started to clear the dishes from the table.

'I'll do this, Lucas. You see to Isobel,' Penny said, standing up to help him.

'Thanks, Penny.'

As father and daughter disappeared upstairs Penny carried the dishes through to the kitchen. She could hear Isobel's laughter drifting down and it made her smile as she stacked the dishwasher.

What would it be like to be a part of their lives? she wondered. To live here as a family? If only she didn't know anything about Lawrence Darien…if only she was here for all the right reasons instead of all the wrong ones. She allowed herself to daydream for a little while and watched the rain outside. It was coming down in thunderous sheets, bouncing off the steps that led up to the veranda.

Flint ambled up to the back door and distracted her as he started whining to get out. 'Are you sure you want to go out there?' Penny asked him. 'It's pretty grim.'

The dog whined again, so she opened the door. Flint took a step back as he saw the rain. 'I did try to warn you.' Penny smiled.

After a moment's hesitation the dog wandered out onto the porch, and a few seconds later he ventured down the steps into the garden. The rain was so heavy it obscured him from view as soon as he had walked a few yards. Penny could hardly even see the car on the drive—it was just a blur of colour against the green grass.

'Flint, come on, boy. Better come back in,' Penny called. But there was no sign of the animal. She stepped out onto the porch. 'Flint!' she called again.

The light was fading now, and darkness was dropping fast. The smell of rain was fresh and heavy in the air, and although it was still warm it was a more bearable temperature than it had been all day.

Penny leaned against the railing and took deep breaths.

'Pleasant out here when it rains, isn't it?' Lucas said from behind her.

She turned and found him watching her from the doorway. 'Yes, it's fresh and quite exhilarating, isn't it? I was just waiting for Flint—he very bravely headed out into the garden.'

'He likes the coolness of this weather.' Lucas walked over to stand beside her. 'I like it myself. It's as if everything is being washed clean, isn't it?'

There was silence for a while, except for the rumble of rain on the roof over their heads. Penny watched as it fell like a watery blanket, enclosing them from the darkness of the world outside.

'Shall we forget our disagreement earlier?' he asked suddenly.

She nodded.

'I don't really think you are sanctimonious. Just a bit irritating and stubborn at times.' He grinned.

'Stubborn?' She turned and looked at him with a raised eyebrow. 'How do you arrive at that conclusion?'

'Well, you won't admit that I'm right—which, of course, I nearly always am,' he said teasingly.

'You wish.' Penny shook her head and looked away from him.

'Penny?'

She looked over at him questioningly.

'Are you okay?'

'Yes—why?'

'You just looked so serious for a moment.'

'I'm fine.'

'Good…I'm glad we are still friends.' The half teasing smile made her heart dip crazily. Maybe here in this house they were friends, but outside in the real world he could never be anything other than her father's enemy. As she looked into his eyes she found herself wishing that they could stay like this for ever, cocooned from reality, that time could stand still and she wouldn't have to leave.

Flint came hurrying back up the steps to the veranda, and then, before they could move out of his way, shook himself vigorously. 'Flint!' they both shouted in dismay as water flew all over them in icy droplets.

'Thanks a bunch, fella,' Lucas said, brushing himself down.

Flint looked up at him with unconcerned eyes and shook himself again, which made Penny laugh because she had wisely moved further away.

'Very funny.' Lucas looked over at her and smiled wryly. 'Look at me—I'm soaked!' He brushed at his white shirt, which was now sticking to him in damp patches.

'That will teach you to think you are always right,' Penny said, laughing again.

'Hey, take that back immediately. I expect a little more meekness and subordination from my employees,' he said laughingly.

'Then I think you've got the wrong employee,' she said with a grin.

'You might be right.' He advanced towards her, a wicked light of indignation in his eyes.

'Anyway, I'd better go and tuck Isobel up,' she said with a smile as she backed away from him.

'Oh, no, you don't...' He caught up with her before she had reached the door and put a hand on the wall behind her, effectively trapping her close to him. 'Before I let you escape I think an apology might be in order.'

'An apology for what?' She smiled. 'Siding with Flint?'

'No, an apology for being volatile and difficult.'

'Difficult! You're the difficult one.' She raised her chin slightly.

'Last chance—you'd better start saying you are sorry, otherwise I just might have to kiss you senseless.' His eyes moved towards her lips and suddenly the mood between them changed dramatically. The laughter and the teasing disappeared, replaced by a powerful surge of sexual awareness.

She moistened her lips nervously; her heart was racing out of control. She wanted him to kiss her...wanted him so much it was as if every inch, every nerve in her body was crying out for him.

As he lowered his head she closed her eyes. The touch of his lips against hers was electric; it sent shivery waves of delight shooting through her. She reached her hands up tentatively and rested them against his shoulders, then slid them higher around his neck and kissed him back with heated passion.

All coherent thought slipped away in those few moments of ecstasy. She felt his hands around her waist and longed for them to caress her, longed to get even closer into his arms.

The sound of the rain seemed to drown out all the voices inside her that said this was wrong.

He was the one to pull back from her, leaving her breathless and filled with a gnawing ache of need inside.

'I suppose we shouldn't have done that,' she whispered unsteadily.

'Why not?' He smiled at her.

'Because…' *Because this was wrong,* her mind screamed. *Because she was lying to him about who she was and they could never have a relationship in any real sense…* The knowledge washed through her in cold waves of torment. 'Because…this will complicate our working relationship,' she finished weakly. 'And, anyway, didn't you just send Emma some flowers? Do you really think it's right to kiss me and pursue her at the same time?'

He smiled. 'Are you jealous, by any chance?'

'No, of course not.' The arrogant question set her blood on fire. But the annoying thing was that he was right. She was jealous of Emma even though she had no earthly right to be.

'Anyway, I'd better go…' She ducked away from him, under his arm. 'I don't want to keep Isobel waiting. Will you ring for a taxi for me while I tuck her in?'

'If that's what you want.'

It wasn't what she wanted; she looked over at him and felt as if her heart was truly breaking. Then hurriedly she went inside.

Isobel was cuddled down beneath the sheets, her teddy bear held tight in her arms. Penny sat down on the bed beside her.

'Thanks for coming shopping with me, Milly,' she said.

'I enjoyed it,' Penny said truthfully. 'And you looked gorgeous in your dress.'

The child nodded. 'I got the best dress in the whole world,' she said solemnly.

'I think you did,' Penny agreed with a smile. She reached out and tenderly stroked a stray strand of hair back from the little girl's face, and as she did so the knowledge that this wasn't goodnight but goodbye swamped her with sadness. 'I'm sure you will be the most beautiful girl in the play.' She bent and kissed her on the forehead. 'Now, time for sleep.'

'Milly, will you come and see me in my play?' The child asked suddenly, before she could stand up.

Penny bit down on her lip. 'I don't think I can, Isobel.'

'Why?' A frown creased the smooth lines of the child's forehead.

'Because...' Penny paused, and then decided it was best to tell the little girl the truth. 'I have to go home and see my dad for a while because he needs me.'

'Oh!' Isobel looked as if she might cry suddenly.

'But that doesn't mean I don't want to come, Issy,' Penny said gently. 'Given the chance I would love to see you in your school play. But sometimes things just aren't possible. I'm worried about my dad, you see, because he's on his own. You do understand, don't you?'

Isobel nodded. 'Like me and my daddy?'

'Yes. A bit like that.' Penny smiled at her. 'But I will be thinking about you and wondering how you are getting on.'

'I'll think about you too,' Isobel said, and cuddled further down next to her teddy bear.

'Shall I switch off this light?' Penny asked as she moved away.

'No…I like the light on.' The child's eyes were growing heavy now. 'See you tomorrow, Milly.'

'Goodnight, Isobel. Sweet dreams.' As she crept from the room she saw Lucas standing in the shadows outside the doorway.

'Why won't you be here for her play?' he asked quietly as he closed the door behind her.

'I told you—I've got to go home.' She started to move away from him towards the stairs. She really felt that she needed to get out of here fairly quickly—because if she didn't she might start crying. Saying goodbye to Isobel had been even harder than she had expected. But before she could move very far Lucas caught hold of her arm.

'You know Isobel's play isn't for another three weeks,' he said crisply. 'I thought you said you'd be back by then?'

'Is it three weeks away?' Penny feigned puzzlement. 'Well, then, I probably will make it. I just didn't want to make promises I might not be able to keep.'

He pulled her around so that she was forced to look at him. 'But you don't mind making promises to me that you can't keep?' His eyes moved searchingly over her face. 'What is going on, Penny?'

'I told you—I'm worried about my father.'

'And that's all?'

'It's enough…believe me.' For a moment her voice was unsteady, and her eyes lingered on his mouth for longer than they should have. 'Did you ring for a taxi for me?'

'What do you think?' he murmured dryly.

'I think you should have done,' she said huskily, but

at the same time she could feel herself swaying closer towards him.

'No, you don't. You think that we have some unfinished business.'

'Down in the office, you mean? Looking through those files…?' She tried to make light of the situation. 'Emma is right about you. You've got a one-track mind for business…'

He ignored the flippant statement and instead leaned closer and touched his lips against hers, tasting her as if she were some rare delicacy that needed savouring. The sensations that flowed through her were bittersweet. She wanted him so much.

'My one-track mind at the moment is firmly focused on you…' he murmured as he pulled back fractionally. 'And don't tell me you don't want me to do this…because I know that you do…you want me as badly as I want you.'

The arrogant confidence of his words was punctuated by the feel of his hands as they moved over her body with assured, masterful strokes. She told herself that she should push him away, but she couldn't. His caresses were sending her body wild with need. She wanted so much more. He was right—she did want him as much as he wanted her.

He bent to take possession of her lips again, and she kissed him back with hungry approval. She felt his hands moving to undress her; the zip at the back of her dress was pulled down, his hand moving beneath to find the cool softness of her skin.

Then he lifted her up and carried her through to the bedroom.

'Now, where were we…?' he said as he placed her down on the bed.

Even as she was telling herself that this was wrong she was reaching to unbutton his shirt with feverish fingers. What difference would one more night make? she asked herself weakly. She just wanted to feel his body against her, relish the heady bliss of his kisses and his caresses one last time. Was that really so wrong? Then she would walk away and put this episode in her life behind her— forget it as best she could...

CHAPTER ELEVEN

PENNY lay in the warm circle of Lucas's arms, her head against his chest, listening to the steady sound of his breathing, the regular beat of his heart. Their passion had been wild and gloriously fulfilling; now, sleepy and sated, they lay wrapped in each other's arms. Outside the rain was still thundering down in relentless torrents. To Penny it sounded like tumultuous applause—probably the heavens' sarcastic approval for another spectacular mistake, she thought with dry irony. She should never have stayed; all she had succeeded in doing was proving to herself how much she loved him, how much she was giving up by walking away.

She would never be able to forget Lucas…never. Turning her head slightly, she looked at the illuminated numbers on the alarm clock next to the bed. If she was to have any chance of catching her flight she would have to leave now.

'Lucas?' She whispered his name, her voice husky in the darkness.

There was no reply.

Cautiously she pulled away from him. His arm tightened around her for a moment and she stopped, fearing he had woken up. But the pattern of his breathing didn't alter. She slipped out from his arms and then looked back at him. The light from the landing was slanting over the bed; the covers were low on his waist, revealing the powerful shoulders, the broad chest. But it was his face that held her attention. She drank in the lean, handsome features for one last time.

Then impulsively she leaned over and kissed him on the lips. He smiled sleepily and reached out, stroking his hand through the silky softness of her hair, pulling her in close against him. For a moment she allowed herself one last luxury of being held by him. Then, taking a deep breath, she moved away.

He didn't stir. Hurriedly she picked up her clothes from the floor, searching under the bed for a shoe that was mysteriously missing. She found it after a few frantic minutes and then tiptoed quietly away.

She got dressed in the lounge at the same time as phoning for a taxi. Then she spent an anxious half an hour waiting for it to arrive whilst penning a short note to Lucas, which she put on the hall table by the phone. It was almost ten by the time she left, closing the door quietly behind her. She had a last glimpse of Lucas's house through the rain-splattered windows of the taxi as it pulled away.

Then she turned and stared resolutely in front of her at the darkness of the country roads. Her father needed her, and her first loyalty had to be to him. There could be no more looking back now. Lucas and Isobel were in the past.

Her flight was delayed, which was good news because otherwise she might have missed it. She arrived at the airport with minutes to spare, but ended up spending nearly the whole night in the departure lounge, staring up at the screens.

It was daylight when she finally touched down in Arbuda. It felt really weird, coming out of the familiar terminal into the heat of the morning. Nothing much changed on this small island—it was as if time had stood still and she had never been away. Even the same taxi drivers sat outside, smoking and laughing as they waited for a fare.

As she climbed into the taxi that would take her on the last leg of her journey she felt tired and edgy. She leaned back and closed her eyes, and memories of Lucas making love to her filtered through her mind. His hands on her body, his lips heated and passionate against hers. What would he think when he woke this morning to find her gone? When he read her note telling him she wouldn't be back and that she was sorry?

She squeezed her eyes tight in an effort not to think about it. At least he would never find out how she had deceived him and who she really was... She had made sure all traces of her name had been scrubbed out of the hotel register before she left. The woman receptionist had been very understanding when she had told her she was running away from a possessive boyfriend and didn't want him to trace her. The man who worked there had looked rather more suspicious when she had said the same thing to him earlier that morning, but she had slipped him a few dollars and he had nodded and shrugged his shoulders. And as they had never had her Arbuda address anyway, just her Miami base address for work, she supposed that her secret was now safe.

Not that Lucas would give her a lot of thought. He'd probably be more bothered that she had left him in the lurch at work than anything else.

As she opened her eyes the taxi pulled into the driveway of her father's house. She noticed the sugar cane was still in the fields.

The house came into view after a few minutes. It looked sadly neglected—the railing to the front door was hanging off and the blue paint that had once looked so pretty on the shutters was fading.

'Have you seen anything of my father recently, Joshua?' Penny asked, leaning forwards to talk to the taxi driver.

'No, miss. He had to lay off some of his labourers, and I heard from Mrs Gillingham that he's been in a bad way. She's been bringing him in a little of her chicken soup, trying to do her best for him.'

Penny's heart missed a beat. If her father was accepting Mrs Gillingham's help he must indeed be in a bad way. Mrs Gillingham was her father's neighbour, a kindly widow who sometimes popped over to see him—much to his annoyance. He couldn't stick her, and complained loudly about her being a very annoying woman.

'Thanks, Joshua.' As soon as the taxi pulled to a halt she jumped out and paid him, and practically ran up to the front door.

'Dad?' she called loudly as she walked through the front door. The place looked surprisingly clean and tidy. Usually when she came home on leave she spent her time cleaning and organising. 'Dad, are you okay?'

The door through to the kitchen opened and Mrs Gillingham came out. She was a plump woman in her sixties, with a pleasant smiling face. 'Oh, it's you, dear; I wondered what the commotion was. Your father is upstairs in his bed. He had an accident a couple of days ago—'

'What kind of an accident? Is he okay?' Penny asked in consternation.

'He had a car crash and broke his leg. Poor man has been in a bit of a state.'

'Oh, no! Thanks, Mrs Gillingham.' Penny took the stairs two at a time to go up and see him.

She found him lying on top of the patchwork counterpane in his bedroom reading a newspaper. He put it down as she came in and she was shocked to see how frail he looked. All colour had gone from his face and he had lost a lot of weight in the few months since she had last been home.

'Dad, are you okay?' She went over to put her arms around him.

He smiled tenderly at her as she pulled back. 'I'm all the better for seeing you. Where have you been? I tried to get in contact with you via your company and they said you were off on leave.'

'I had a bit of business to deal with,' Penny said guiltily. 'You could have phoned me on my mobile.'

'I've lost the number—don't know what the heck I've done with my address book.'

'Oh, Dad, what am I going to do with you?'

'Worse than that, I think I've lost the house, Penny,' he said sadly.

'Have you received the eviction order?'

Her father shook his head. 'But it's only a matter of time. I can't afford these massive repayments that Darien insisted on. And I've had to lay off workers, which means I won't get the sugar crop in time, which means I'm even further behind.'

'I'm sorry, Dad,' Penny said softly, her heart going out to him.

'It's not your fault.' He smiled sadly. 'It's my own, for getting involved with Lawrence Darien. That man never forgave me for stealing your mother away from him.'

'Well, you didn't exactly steal her. She found out he was married and finished with him.'

William Kennedy inclined his head. 'But she found out

he was married because I told her.' His lips twisted
wryly. 'I played a bit dirty, I suppose.'

'He was still married—he was the one playing dirty.'

'Well, whatever... He never did forgive me. And now
it seems his son is just as cold as he was.'

Penny thought about Lucas. 'Cold' wasn't how she
would ever describe him. 'You don't really know that for
a fact, Dad.'

Her father looked at her with sceptical eyes. 'That guy
is a chip off the old block. If I ever saw him I'd—' For
a moment her father's face seemed to heat up to a shade
of purple that wasn't healthy.

'Now, now, William...' Mrs Gillingham strolled in
with a tray. 'You're not upsetting yourself, are you?' She
put the tray down beside him and reached to plump up
the pillows at his back.

'Don't fuss, woman,' he said with agitation. 'I'm fine.'

'No, you're not—you are getting your blood pressure
up for no reason at all.'

'Your blood pressure would be up if you were losing
your house,' William muttered.

Rona Gillingham rolled her eyes at Penny. 'You just
concentrate on eating that sandwich and getting well. I'll
pop back later to see how you are going on.'

'I'll be fine now that Penny is here,' William said in
a low tone.

'Well, I'll pop in later anyway.' With a smile, the
woman retreated.

'Thanks, Mrs Gillingham,' Penny called after her, but
she had already gone.

'You shouldn't be so tetchy, Dad. You are very lucky
to have such a nice neighbour,' she said crossly as she
passed him over his tray.

'She's never been away from here, you know...

morning, noon and night.' He reached to pick up the sandwich on the tray, then added softly. 'Fine woman, though…fine woman.'

'Dad?' Penny looked over at him in surprise and then smiled. 'There's life in the old dog yet, isn't there? Despite that plaster on your leg.'

Her father grinned. 'If I could just forget about Darien I'd be happy,' he muttered dryly.

'I don't think there is much chance of that, Dad. But I'm home now, and I have another few weeks leave ahead of me. I'll help you pack everything up.'

'You will not. I'm not packing anything until I have to.' William leaned back against the pillows. 'But if you'd organise the remainder of my workforce to help bring the sugar in, I'd be very grateful. Who knows? We might get the harvest in on time after all.'

'You mean if I work day and night?' Penny looked over at him and shook her head.

'Oh, go on, Pen…for your dear old dad. Just think— we might be able to teach that Darien ogre a thing or two after all, like don't underestimate a Kennedy.'

Despite the breeze, the temperature was sizzling. Penny had brought drinks down to the workers in the fields, and now she sat down in the field of sugar cane and looked up at the blue sky.

It was nearly two weeks now since she had left Puerto Rico, and surprisingly no eviction notice had arrived. In fact, no communication from Lucas had arrived at all. Planning permission would be revoked in two days. She wondered what on earth was going on. Had something happened to Lucas? Maybe he was ill…? Maybe Isobel was ill and everything was just forgotten as he dealt with the problem?

She closed her eyes and tried to rid herself of the idea that had been lurking in the cold depths of her thoughts for a few days now. Lucas would be fine…and so would Isobel, she tried to reassure herself. They would probably hear from him today, and by tomorrow a JCB would arrive to start digging foundations.

A breeze rustled through the sugar cane around her. God, she missed him… Every day she thought of him, remembered the way he had kissed her, held her…looked at her. As a treat she allowed herself to conjure him up in her mind, tall and lithe, with those powerful shoulders. She remembered how it had felt to be held in the tenderness of his embrace. The way he'd half smiled sometimes, and the way he'd watched her with those dark, incredibly sexy eyes.

There was the sound of a car pulling up by the gates further down from her. Penny didn't stand up to investigate. She was dreamily imagining she was lying in Lucas's arms.

Somebody got out of the car and called to one of the workmen standing nearby.

'Afternoon—I'm looking for the William Kennedy residence.'

The familiar husky timbre of the voice made Penny's heart stop beating for an instant. It sounded like Lucas! Was she conjuring him up so vividly in her mind that she was imagining his voice?

She sat up, and through the dense screen of sugar cane she could just make out a tall man standing by the side of the road. He had his back to her, but he had a similar build to Lucas and dark hair. He was wearing khaki trousers and a matching short-sleeved shirt.

She saw her co-worker Matthew pointing up the drive towards her father's house. The man turned to get back in his car, and Penny felt the world tip at a dizzying crazy angle as she realised it was indeed Lucas Darien. For a moment she was just so incredibly pleased to see him that she couldn't think of anything else. But as he got back into the red sports car and turned up the drive her brain suddenly started to click into gear again.

What on earth did he want? Was he coming to take possession of the property in person, rather than sending in the bailiffs? The notion made fear zing through her veins. That would be enough to give her father a heart attack.

She scrambled quickly to her feet to try and stop him, but she was too late. He had already driven past her, leaving a white trail of dust in his wake.

'Matthew!' She called across to her colleague as he turned his attention back to lancing through the cane. 'What did that man want?'

'He was looking for your father. Has some business with him.' Matthew shook his head. 'He didn't say what it was about.'

'Damn!' Penny took a deep breath. She was going to have to get back to the house, and quick. Only trouble was their other colleague Jim had just driven off with the truck ten minutes earlier. There was nothing else for it— she had to set off at a run up the drive. She took a short-cut across the fields halfway up, but it still took her half an hour to reach the house.

Just in time to see Lucas driving off looking rather grim-faced. He didn't see her, however; he was too busy turning the car before heading back down the drive.

Penny entered the house, her heart racing, her mouth dry with fear as she wondered what kind of state she would find her father in.

He was sitting in the lounge, staring out of the window with a strangely silent look about him.

'Dad?' Penny approached cautiously. 'What was that all about? Is everything all right?'

'Hmm?' William Kennedy looked over at his daughter with a faraway expression on his face.

'Was that Lucas Darien?'

'Yes...very strange...'

'What's strange?' Penny came closer. 'What happened, Dad?'

'He apologised to me.' Her father raised his eyes towards hers. 'Can you believe it? Told me that he was calling off his solicitor and that the house was mine.'

Penny sat down on the adjacent chair, her legs weak with relief. 'Why?'

'Seems when he was going through his father's files he found a codicil to the will. Lawrence had had second thoughts about pursuing his vendetta against me.' William held up a letter. 'He'd even left a letter for me, written to me on his deathbed, telling me he regretted his actions...that he had been obsessed with Clara and had never got over losing her...'

'Really?' Penny was stunned. 'What did Lucas say?'

'Well, he hadn't read the letter. It was sealed and addressed to me, and he said he felt he should deliver it in person. He also handed me a cheque to cover my losses and he apologised profusely.' William shrugged. 'I was going to make a fuss—tell him what I thought...but I found I couldn't because... Well, he is a very decent chap, actually...who'd have thought it...eh?'

'Did he mention me?' Penny asked, her heart thundering nervously.

'You?' William frowned. 'Why would he mention you?'

Why, indeed, when he didn't even know of her con-
nection here? Penny bit down on her lip. 'I didn't tell
you, Dad, but I went to see him.'

Her father looked at her as if only just seeing her for
the first time. 'Oh!' Then he smiled. 'Is he the reason
you've been looking so damn miserable these last few
weeks?'

Penny nodded.

'Well, you'd better get after him, hadn't you? He's
staying in town tonight, at the Sheraton hotel. He leaves
first thing tomorrow morning.'

Penny scrambled to her feet and ran out of the room.
It was only when she got into the hall that she caught
sight of herself in the mirror. She was wearing faded blue
jeans and a rather clingy old white T-shirt. Maybe she
had better change first, she thought.

It was strange whilst she was showering and changing
and getting ready to go after Lucas. Her adrenalin was
running high with feverish excitement. It was only after
she had parked her father's battered old pick-up truck a
few blocks down from the swish hotel building that she
started to have doubts…that excitement turned to nerves.

Going after Lucas was all very well, but just say he
wasn't interested… Maybe he hadn't even missed her.
He might even be back with Emma by now.

She stepped out of the car and brushed a nervous hand
down over her blue dress. What should she say to him?
Even though he had discovered the truth about his father
it couldn't be easy for him. He probably wasn't in the
best of moods, and finding out that she was William
Kennedy's daughter might really infuriate him.

The sun was setting in a flamingo-pink sky as Penny
walked slowly up to the front entrance to the hotel. Gold
lights illuminated the impressive lobby. It's now or never,

Penny told herself firmly. If she didn't go in and talk to Lucas she would always wonder about what might have been.

As she walked in towards the reception desk a man walked out from one of the lounges and preceded her to the desk. Penny was so busy rehearsing in her mind what she would say to Lucas that she didn't pay him much attention.

It was only when the receptionist smiled and said, 'Evening, Mr Darien,' that Penny realised it was Lucas, who was now standing with his back to her a few yards away.

'Evening, Dominique—any messages for me?' He sounded his usual nonchalant self, but just the deep, familiar resonances of his tone made Penny's emotions dissolve with longing.

'Two phone calls, sir.' The woman handed across a piece of paper from one of the pigeonholes behind him.

'Thanks.' Smiling, Lucas turned—and that was when his gaze connected with Penny's.

The first thing Penny noted was the look of complete surprise in his dark eyes.

'Penny—what the heck are you doing here?' he grated, a raw tone to his voice.

'I live here,' she said quietly 'I—'

'What? In the Sheraton Hotel, Arbuda?' he said sarcastically. 'What do you do? Skip around the Caribbean using different aliases for different islands?'

'Don't be silly—'

'Silly?' His eyes narrowed on her and she realised she had said the wrong thing. He advanced slowly and with each step she felt her heart thudding with nerves. There was no mistaking the fact that he was angry with her...blazing, in fact. 'What the hell are you playing at?'

Have you any idea how I felt when I found that damn note you left?'

'I had to go, Lucas…' She shook her head helplessly.

'Without even a word?' He shook his head and then he grabbed hold of her arm, his fingers squeezing into her skin.

'I tried to tell you I had to leave, but you didn't want to listen—'

'Well, I'm listening now.' He marched her firmly across the foyer.

'Where are we going?'

'We're going somewhere private, where you can explain yourself.' He stopped by the lifts and pushed a button for the doors to open. Then he marched her into the mirrored interior.

Another couple stepped in beside them just as the door was about to close. There was silence as the elevator swept smoothly up towards the top floor. Surreptitiously Penny studied Lucas in the smoked mirrors. She had never seen him look so tense. Even on the morning when Mildred Bancroft arrived he hadn't seemed this formidable!

The lift stopped and the other couple got out. They continued upwards.

'Lucas, will you let go of me?' she murmured, looking down at the hand on her arm.

'I don't feel like letting go of you,' he grated. 'You've got some explaining to do.' The doors swished open and he steered her outside into the long, empty corridor.

'Look, I know I've got explaining to do—that's why I'm here… You don't need to frog-march me like this.'

But still Lucas didn't let go of her. She watched as he put a security card into one of the doors and pushed it open. Then they walked in to a sumptuous apartment. It had gold carpets and deep sofas in heavy brocade material. There were double patio doors at one end, that were open to a balcony overlooking the velvet darkness of the Caribbean Sea. The tranquil scene, bathed by the silvery light of a full moon, was very much at odds with the tense atmosphere between them in the room.

'Okay, you said you wanted to explain—now explain,' Lucas said tersely as he released her.

'Lucas, don't be like this.' She rubbed at her arm absently.

'How do you expect me to be?' His eyes were cold.

She pushed a shaking hand through her long blonde hair. 'You've got every right to be angry, I know that.'

'Good.' His eyes flicked over her, taking in the high heels, the tanned long legs and the stylish way her dress emphasised the perfect proportions of her figure. 'Because I'm not just angry, I'm furious. So where the hell have you been?'

'I told you I had to come home, that my father needed me.' There was a heartbeat of a pause before she added softly, 'My father is William Kennedy. You came to see him today. I'm Penny Kennedy.'

'You are William Kennedy's daughter?' His eyes narrowed on her face in a moment of disbelief.

'Yes.' She sat down on the arm of one of the sofas. 'The real reason I came to see you in Puerto Rico was to beg for some leniency for my father.' She flicked an uncertain glance over at him to see how he was taking this, but it was hard to tell. It was as if shutters had come down across his features, leaving just a steely aloofness.

'I never intended to stay…or to deceive you,' she added quickly. 'It was just when you accused my dad of being a no-hoper…a useless reprobate—'

'I never said that,' Lucas cut in, his tone heavy.

'You may as well have.' She glanced over at him. 'It was what you thought, and it made me so damned mad.'

'Indeed,' Lucas murmured coolly.

'Anyway…' Penny carried on uncertainly, flicking an imaginary crease from her dress, not able to look at him properly now. 'When you told me you had to find the deeds to the property before the end of the month I had this idea that if I could find them first it would stop the building work, and also give my father more time to make an interim payment and take some of the pressure off.'

'So you were doing a bit of conservation work as well as a bit of spying for your father?' he grated sardonically.

'Come on, Lucas, give me a break here.' She glanced over at him pleadingly. 'In the end I didn't do anything wrong… In fact, I was more of a help than a hindrance—you've got to admit that.'

'Do I?' Lucas shook his head. 'On the contrary, I think you have been a damned hindrance.'

She bit down on her lip. 'Well, I am sorry you feel like that…but what you were doing was wrong—'

'I was simply following the terms of my father's will. He had made me an executor and I was fulfilling my final obligation to him.'

'Yes, well, your motives weren't completely altruistic; you did stand to make a lot of money from the sale of my father's property to a builder.'

'Is that what you think of me? That my main concern is money?' His voice was cold.

Penny frowned. 'No…' She admitted softly. 'It's not what I think of you at all.'

'You've got to understand, Penny, that my father and I never really saw eye to eye. I knew he was a woman-ser…knew also that he had indulged in some shady deals over the years. But we had patched up our differences before he died and I was glad of that.' Lucas pushed a hand through the darkness of his hair. 'He apologised to me before he died, said how much he regretted some of his actions. He asked me to take charge of his business affairs, said he wanted to leave most of his fortune to me. When I said I didn't want it or need it, he said that I was to accept it for Isobel. That he wanted to make amends for not being around much for her.' He shrugged helplessly. 'What could I say to that? So I agreed, and I tried to do everything strictly by the book. I got rid of his shady solicitor, looked into every aspect of his finances. I had no idea that the repossession order was a personal matter.'

'I know you didn't.'

He met her eyes levelly. 'You should have said something.'

'I didn't think it would do any good. And it wasn't just because you stood to make a lot of money out of the deal. How could I tell you that your father was...?' She glanced over at him warily. It was one thing for him to criticise his father, but quite another for her to do it. 'That he hadn't been particularly kind...' She finished weakly. 'I couldn't do it, Lucas, and then I got firmly enmeshed in the lies and became too nervous about telling you the truth.'

'Really?' One dark eyebrow lifted wryly.

'Yes, really.' She looked over at him steadily. 'I didn't want you to hate me...'

'So you just ran away?'

'I didn't run away. I just had to leave.' She swallowed hard. 'Don't you understand, Lucas? You were my father's enemy. And I'm all he's got.' Her green eyes held his earnestly. 'He's been through hell, worrying about losing his house, how could I tell him he was also losing me—that I'd taken up with the enemy?' Her voice trembled. 'The state he was in, it would have finished him off.'

'He's a lucky man to have someone so loyal to him,' Lucas said quietly.

'I didn't feel very loyal sometimes,' she murmured huskily, and then blushed as he looked over and met her eyes. 'Anyway…' She looked away from him hastily. 'I hope you'll forgive me.'

Lucas didn't say anything for a long moment, and Penny felt her nerves twist with unmerciful anxiety. 'Would you like a drink?' he asked finally, and turned away to the mini-bar behind him.

Was that all he was going to say? Penny stared at him in frustration. 'No. I've got to drive home.'

She watched as he poured himself a whisky.

'So this is home, is it?' he asked, turning to look at her again.

For a second Penny had a vivid image of sitting at Lucas's dining table, with the candlelight flickering between them and Isobel complaining that she would have preferred chips. She remembered standing in the kitchen, looking out at the rain and listening to the child's laughter upstairs as Lucas teased her about something. There had been a warm feeling of belonging in that house, the feeling of being a part of a family. She ached for that almost as much as she ached for Lucas to put his arms around her.

'This is home sometimes,' she said huskily. 'But I don't live here. I'm manageress of a beauty spa on board a cruise ship.'

Lucas watched the golden liquid swirl around the crystal glass. 'You are full of surprises, Ms Kennedy.'

Penny felt a lump wedge in her throat. It didn't sound as if Lucas would ever forgive her.

'And you made a hell of a PA,' he remarked casually.

Penny frowned. 'I was good at that job,' she said with a flash of annoyance, her old spirit returning. She glared at him. 'You know I was. I'm computer literate, and I can run an office like yours no problem.'

'Yes. That's what I said; you were a hell of a PA. How come you were so proficient in an office when it's not really your line?'

'I did an office management course years ago.' She shrugged, not really wanting to talk about such mundane things. But as silence stretched between them she found herself filling the space with more mundane conversation. 'Have you got someone else to replace me?'

'Why? Do you want your job back?' He grinned suddenly.

'No, I just wondered.' She frowned, wishing she hadn't asked. 'I've got my own job, and it's very rewarding. Honestly, you can be damned arrogant sometimes,' she muttered.

'If you really want to know I've missed you like crazy.' He finished his drink and put the empty glass down.

She glanced over at him, her heart unsteady now as she wondered if he was talking in a business sense or a personal one. 'Even though a moment ago you were telling me I was a damned hindrance?' She managed to sound slightly sardonic.

'You were.' He met her eyes levelly. 'You were a damn distraction.'

Her heart started to race as he walked across toward

her. 'You are a distraction now. Sometimes I can hardly think straight when I look at you...do you know that?'

She looked up at him, unsure what direction his words were taking.

'You see, that's exactly what I'm talking about.' He shook his head. 'You look at me with those gorgeous eyes and things start to fragment in my mind... It happened the first day you walked into my office.' He reached out and caught hold of her hand, pulling her to her feet. 'I knew I should have asked you more questions—especially as I knew full well your CV wasn't right. But all I could think was...I want this woman to stay.'

Penny's heart leapt wildly.

'That feeling hasn't happened to me in a very long time,' he finished huskily, his eyes on her lips.

'Hasn't it?' She took a deep breath. 'If you want to know the truth, something happened to me that day too. I walked in and you looked at me and I almost forgot why I was there. I think that was part of the reason why I fell so easily into the lie of being Mildred Bancroft.'

'And then you left with equal ease. Have you any idea how I felt when I woke up and found you were gone? When I found that note?' His voice hardened.

She opened her mouth to answer, but suddenly she was in his arms and he was kissing her with a punishing degree of passion. She clung to him, excitement and need racing like fire through her veins as she kissed him back.

'I didn't want to go, Lucas...I really didn't,' she breathed unsteadily, wrapping her arms up around his neck, hardly daring to believe that he was kissing her, that he seemed to have forgiven her. 'I'm sorry...I'm sorry.' She punctuated the words with kisses, trailing her fingers through the soft darkness of his hair, loving the feeling of being so close, of being able to touch him…love him.

'No, I'm sorry,' he murmured, kissing her back, his hands travelling up and over her body with slow, sensuous strokes. 'Sorry I ever let you escape so easily. I can see now that I'm going to have to do something very radical about that…'

She pulled away from him, a small frown over her eyes.

'And I can also see that I'm going to have to do something about the fact that you keep changing your name.'

'I'm not going to change my name again, Lucas. Penny Kennedy is my name—I thought we'd cleared the air—'

'We have.' He kissed the tip of her nose, and then the frown from between her eyes. 'I just think that to be on the safe side we should change it again—this time more permanently.'

'Lucas, what are you talking about?' She pulled further away from him.

'I'm talking about changing your name to Mrs Lucas Darien,' he said softly. 'I want you to marry me, Penny…that way I hope that I can ensure you will stay around every day and every night for the rest of my life.'

She was so stunned she could hardly speak. He watched as the colour drained from her face.

'Penny?'

'Why are you asking me this?' she asked huskily.

'Because I'm in love with you.' He answered her with deep sincerity. 'And I don't want to lose you ever again.'

The words made her mind reel with happiness, with disbelief. She stared up at him wordlessly for a few seconds and then her eyes filled with tears. 'I thought…I wondered if you were seeing Emma again…'

'Why would you think that?'

Penny shrugged awkwardly. 'Because you sent her flowers...because Maria said you'd been the happiest she had known you in a long time when you were dating her.'

'Emma was only ever just a friend. She wanted more from me than I could give her. The flowers were sent out of friendship, for her birthday, and I made it clear there was no other motive.' He said the words steadily and reached to pull her close again. 'She's a very nice person, but just not right for me. In fact I had given up ever finding the right person again...until you walked into my office.'

A tear trickled down the smooth paleness of her skin. In these weeks apart from him she had dreamed of this, yearned for it, but she had never dared hope it would ever be possible.

'Look, I know you have a fabulous job...and I know you value your freedom...but if you say yes, Penny, I will do everything in my power to make you happy. The fact is I'm crazy about you...no other reason in the world would make me propose.'

'Oh, Lucas.' Her voice wobbled precariously. 'I'm crazy about you too...I adore you. I think I fell in love with you the first moment I saw you.'

She saw the light of happiness in his eyes as she said those words, and suddenly she was crushed in his arms and he was kissing her with such passion that it took her breath away. She clung to him, kissing him back, joy flooding through her with fierce intensity.

'I can't believe this is happening,' she whispered as he pulled back slightly to look at her.

'Neither can I. I didn't think I could ever feel this happy again.'

'I know.' She bit down on her lip.

'Hey, wait until Isobel hears our news—she's going to be ecstatic.'

The words caused a flood of warmth and excitement to rush through her. 'I've missed Isobel so much...how is she?'

'Fine—she's spending time with her grandma, but I've got to be back tomorrow.' He looked down at her earnestly. 'You will come back with me, won't you?'

She nodded. 'Try and stop me,' she whispered softly. 'As Shauna said, when you meet the man you want to spend the rest of your life with you want the rest of your life to start straight away...'

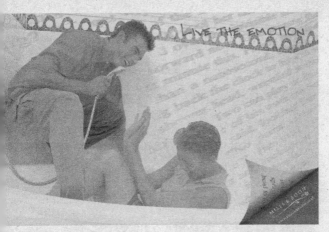

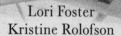

FREE!

4 Books
and a surprise gift!

We would like to take this opportunity to thank you for reading this Mills & Boon® book by offering you the chance to take FOUR more specially selected titles from the Modern Romance™ series absolutely FREE! We're also making this offer to introduce you to the benefits of the Reader Service™—

- ★ FREE home delivery
- ★ FREE gifts and competitions
- ★ FREE monthly Newsletter
- ★ Books available before they're in the shops
- ★ Exclusive Reader Service discount

Accepting these FREE books and gift places you under no obligation to buy; you may cancel at any time, even after receiving your free shipment. Simply complete your details below and return the entire page to the address below. *You don't even need a stamp!*

YES! Please send me 4 free Modern Romance books and a surprise gift. I understand that unless you hear from me, I will receive 6 superb new titles every month for just £2.69 each, postage and packing free. I am under no obligation to purchase any books and may cancel my subscription at any time. The free books and gift will be mine to keep in any case.

P4ZEE

Ms/Mrs/Miss/Mr ....Initials...
BLOCK CAPITALS PLEASE

Surname..

Address...

....

....Postcode ....

Send this whole page to:
UK: The Reader Service, FREEPOST CN81, Croydon, CR9 3WZ
EIRE: The Reader Service, PO Box 4546, Kilcock, County Kildare (stamp required)